ERLE STANLEY GARDNER

- Cited by the *Guinness Book of World Records* as the #1 bestselling writer of all time!

- Author of more than 150 clever, authentic, and sophisticated mystery novels!

- Creator of the amazing Perry Mason, the savvy Della Street, and dynamite detective Paul Drake!

- THE ONLY AUTHOR WHO OUT-SELLS AGATHA CHRISTIE, HAROLD ROBBINS, BARBARA CARTLAND, AND LOUIS L'AMOUR *COMBINED!*

Why?

Because he writes the best, most fascinating whodunits of all!

You'll want to read every one of them, from
BALLANTINE BOOKS

Also by Erle Stanley Gardner
Published by Ballantine Books:

The Case of the
Cautious Coquette

Erle Stanley Gardner

BALLANTINE BOOKS • NEW YORK

Foreword and dedication

All of my life I have fought for the underdog and tried to improve the administration of justice.

I am assuming that the readers of this book are interested in crime and in justice.

I am hoping that this foreword can call attention to one of the great injustices of our day.

When a criminal's sentence has expired he walks down the front steps of the penitentiary a free man. Theoretically he has paid his dept to society and is on his way to sin no more. Actually in far too many cases an embittered, deadly enemy of society is walking out without any restraining influence whatever, ready to start a new series of depredations.

Parole boards recognize this fact.

When a man is paroled before his sentence expires society has some control over him. He must report to his parole officer. He is placed in some position of gainful employment on his release, and he is supposed to remain on that job and report periodically. If he doesn't do that, he has violated his parole and can be returned to prison.

It is, therefore, patently obvious that even in the most desperate cases it is far better to place *any* prison inmate who shows *any* signs of rehabilitation on parole than to hold him to the last minute of his sentence and then let him vanish into our crowded civilization, subject to no restraining influence, to engage in activities over which the authorities can have no control, and about which they have no knowledge.

Therefore, parole boards, who understand these facts, try to use the power of parole which is vested in them to protect society as much as possible and at the same time give the prison inmate at least an opportunity to engage in legitimate, gainful employment when he is released.

When the parolee makes good the public never hears about the case. The public doesn't know that John Doe, who is giving them such courteous, efficient service in the filling station, is a man who made a mistake, paid his debt to society, and is now on his way up once more.

But when a parolee does commit another crime the public certainly does hear about it. Then there is a hue and cry, a clamor. The parole board is put on the grid and taken to pieces.

Undoubtedly there are many men paroled who shouldn't be paroled. For every such failure, however, there are a dozen successes.

The main point is, the public doesn't realize that virtually all of these men who have been paroled and again violate the law would have been discharged anyway within a relatively brief period.

In the face of this widespread public misunderstanding, in the face of this adverse, unfair smearing in the press, parole boards continue to exercise their best discretion, to study the cases carefully and do their duty as they see it.

Many times these parole boards have but little discretion because the prisons are filled to overflowing. With taxpayers indifferent to the problem, refusing to expand prison facilities, with law enforcement officers sending a constantly increasing stream of new inmates to prison, it is simply a mathematical necessity to let some men out in order to make way for the new men who are coming in. In some instances parole boards make costly mistakes. Human nature being what it is, human judgement being as fallible as human judgment must always be, the only wonder is that they don't make more.

By and large our parole boards are doing a good job.

So by this foreword I wish to pay tribute to a group of men who are courageously continuing to do their duty as they see it. I wish to dedicate this book to the greatest underdog of all in the field of public relations:

The Parole Board

Cast of Characters

Chapter 1

Promptly at nine o'clock, Perry Mason joined Paul Drake for breakfast.

The tall detective, head of the Drake Detective Agency, grinned at the lawyer, said, "You're thirty seconds late, Perry."

Mason shook his head. "Your watch is thirty seconds fast. Have you ordered?"

"I've ordered," Drake said. "Double pineapple juice, ham and eggs, toast and coffee. It'll be coming right up. Have you seen my ad in the paper?"

"No," Mason said. "What ad?"

"In that Finchley case."

"I was going to ask you about that."

"I have an ad in the morning papers. I also have one that came out in the *Blade* yesterday afternoon."

The waiter, entering the booth with the pineapple juice, said, "Good morning, Mr. Mason. Mr. Drake told me to go right ahead and put your order on the stove. The ham and eggs will be right up. He said you'd be here."

"I'm here."

Drake took a long drink of the pineapple juice, then put down the half empty glass, reached in his brief case and took out a newspaper. "Here it is," he said.

Mason looked at the classified ad indicated by the detective.

ONE HUNDRED DOLLARS REWARD!! If the parties who were changing a tire on an automobile at the intersection of

Hickman Avenue and Vermesillo Drive at about five o'clock on the afternoon of the third will communicate with the Drake Detective Agency and give a description sufficient to identify the black sedan which was speeding east on Vermesillo Drive and crashed into the Ford going north on Hickman Avenue they will receive one hundred dollars, cash. Bystanders think the young woman in this parked car jotted down the license number of the speeding sedan but left the scene before the ambulance arrived. Any information from anyone leading to an identification of this hit-and-run driver will result in the prompt payment of one hundred dollars. Address all communications Drake Detective Agency, Box 624.

"That should produce some results," Mason said, putting down the folded newspaper. "That Finchley kid was badly hurt . . . I hate a hit-and-run driver."

"Probably he'd had a few cocktails and didn't dare to stick around," Drake said. "Of course the people in that parked automobile may not have seen anything."

"As I get the story, they did," Mason told him. "There were a man and a woman in the car. It was a light-colored sedan, fairly new. They'd evidently just finished changing a tire. The man was putting the flat tire back in the trunk when the accident happened. The woman wrote something down in a notebook. Apparently it was the license number of the automobile that speeded away from the scene of the accident after slamming the Finchley Ford over against the lamppost."

The waiter brought ham and eggs, coffee, golden brown toast.

"Suppose their testimony should be adverse to your clients?" Drake asked.

"It can't be if they're telling the truth. I want to know who they are, anyhow. I don't want them held in the background where they might show up someday as surprise witnesses, testifying on behalf of the defendant."

The waiter popped his head back into the booth and said apologetically, "Your office is on the line, Mr. Drake. Your secretary said I was to tell you there'd been a reply to that ad in the paper, and that you'd want to know about it while you were breakfasting with Mr. Mason."

"Have someone bring the reply down here," Drake said. "Tell my secretary to put a messenger in a taxicab and rush it down here."

Mason grinned. "Shows what advertising will do, Paul."

"Shows what *money* will do," Drake commented.

"That Finchley boy has a broken hip," Mason said. "He was planning on graduating from college. I'd sure like to stick the driver of that car."

Drake sipped coffee, and said wearily, "It probably won't work out that way, Perry. The driver of the other car was drunk. If you could have nabbed him at the scene of the accident, you could have proved he was drunk. The way it is now, he'll have a beautiful fairy story about how the Finchley car crashed into him, that he looked back and felt certain there was no damage done . . ."

"And then I'll tear into him on a hit-and-run charge," Mason said.

Drake grinned. "You just *think* you will. You'll find that the chap has an influential friend or two who has rung up the district attorney. You'll find influential people all over town who'll get busy on the telephone telling what a fine chap he is, good to his family, considerate of his dogs and cats, a person who makes substantial donations to religious causes and to the right political party."

"Nevertheless, I'll tear into him," Mason said. "I'll get him on the witness stand and rip him wide open."

"You won't even get to do that," Drake said. "A representative of some insurance company will get around to Bob Finchley and say, 'Look, if you go to court, even if you recover a big judgment, you'll have a lot of lawyers' bills to pay, and by the time you get done, you'll have all the uncertainty of a lawsuit, you'll have to fight clean through

3

to the Supreme Court, and the net result to you wouldn't be half as good as though we took over and paid all the doctor and hospital bills and gave you a little money that you could put into a new car. In fact, by using connections we have, we can get you one of the late models . . .' "

"Shut up," Mason interrupted, grinning. "You're spoiling my breakfast."

"I was just telling you how it'll go," Drake said.

"I know how it'll go," Mason told him, "but you let me find out who was driving that black sedan and I'll give him something to think about, anyway."

They ate for a while in silence. The waiter appeared once more. "A messenger from your office, Mr. Drake. He said I was to give you this envelope and ask you if he should wait for any instructions."

"No," Drake said. "This letter should speak for itself."

Drake slit open the Manila envelope, which had been sent through the mail addressed to the Drake Detective Agency, said, "There's something heavy in it, Perry."

Drake shook the envelope over the table. A key fell out on the tablecloth.

Drake looked at it with surprise.

"Probably the key to the situation," Mason said.

"*Don't* do that so early in the morning!" Drake told him, wincing.

"What's the letter?" Mason asked.

Leaving the key on the tablecloth, Drake pulled out the letter, typewritten in elite type on a good grade of tinted stationery.

"It's dated yesterday," Drake said, "and is addressed to the Drake Detective Agency. Here's the letter, Perry:

Gentlemen:
The party whose aid you are requesting in your ad in this evening's *Blade* will never get in touch with you voluntarily. Because I am interested in fair play, I am going to give you the following information.

At the time of that accident yesterday afternoon at the intersection of Hickman Avenue and Vermesillo Drive, Lucille Barton and a man, whose name I do not know, had just finished changing a tire on Miss Barton's automobile, a light tan sedan. This automobile was parked on the south side of Vermesillo Drive immediately east of the intersection with Hickman Avenue. Miss Barton saw the accident and with great presence of mind wrote down the license number of the sedan which was speeding away to the east on Vermesillo Drive.

Later on she told her companion what she had done. The man became panic-stricken, explaining to her that it would ruin him if it should be known he was with her at that time. (I have been unable to find out who this man is, or the reason he is so afraid of having his identity known.) However, I am a very good friend of Lucille's. I know that this is a matter which is bothering her conscience. Under the circumstances, she cannot give you the information you wish, nor can she ever admit that she was anywhere near the scene of the accident. I have, however, obtained a duplicate key to her apartment which is at 719 South Gondola. (She is living in Apartment 208.) This is a small apartment house with an outer door, the latch of which can be released by tenants of any of the apartments by means of a button. The key to any of the apartments in the house will fit the outer door. If you will use the enclosed key and go to that apartment sometime between the hours of two o'clock and five o'clock in the afternoon of the fifth, you will find no one in the apartment. There is a writing desk in the northeast corner of the sitting room. If you will look in the upper right-hand pigeonhole of that desk you will find a leather-backed notebook. On the next to the last page of that notebook you will find the license number of the automobile that you want. After you have fully satisfied yourself that this is correct and have determined that this automobile is indeed the one you want, I will make arrangements to get in touch with you, redeem the key and will then expect to be reimbursed in the amount of the one hundred dollars which you have offered for a reward.

Very sincerely yours,
A FRIEND

Drake looked at Mason, said, "Of all the cockeyed things."

"Any handwriting at all?" Mason asked.

"Not a bit. The signature is in typewriting, the same as the letter."

"Let me take a look at it," Mason said.

Drake passed Mason the letter.

"That's a ragged job of typing, Paul," Mason said. "The letters are spaced irregularly, the keys weren't struck with a uniform touch, there are a couple of strikeovers—altogether, I would say, the work of an amateur typist."

Drake nodded. "It looks like a two-finger job. Lots of speed though. That's where the skips and uneven spacing come from. What do you make of it?"

"I'm darned if I know," Mason told him. "It looks like a trap to me. We'll let Della Street cast her feminine eye over it and see what she thinks."

Mason picked up the key, inspected it, saw the number "208" stamped on it, dropped it into his vest pocket and said, "However, it's a lead we can't afford to pass up."

Drake said, with sudden apprehension, "Don't go messing around that apartment, Perry. That's dangerous. If anyone should catch you snooping around in there they could . . ."

"Could what?" Mason asked, smiling. "In order to constitute a burglary, the entrance must be made for a felonious purpose, or . . ."

"Or," Drake said, significantly, "someone could mistake you for a housebreaker, shoot first, and ask questions afterwards."

"But," Mason told him, "you certainly don't expect me to pass up this lead, do you?"

Drake pushed back his plate and picked up the check. "Hell, no," he said, "Do you want to pay the exact amount of this check at the present time, Perry, or have it presented on my expense account later on and take a chance that the amount will be about ten per cent higher at that time?"

6

Mason took the check, said with a grin, "I think it will be a damn sight smarter to pay it now . . . That letter bothers me, Paul. If it were on the up-and-up the writer would have copied the license number from the notebook and asked for the hundred bucks."

"It's a trap of some sort," Drake said.

"Well the bait interests me, Paul."

"That's the theory on which traps are constructed," Drake said.

Chapter 2

Della Street, Perry Mason's confidential secretary, had placed mail in three piles on the lawyer's desk. The *"important"* pile was squarely and suggestively in the middle of the blotter.

Mason, entering through the door which led directly to his private office, removed his latchkey, grinned at Della Street and then frowned at the position of the mail on the desk.

"Hi, Della."

"Good morning," she said. "You've seen Paul Drake?"

"Yes."

"His office was trying to get in touch with us. I knew you were having breakfast with him."

Mason hung up his hat, regarded the pile of mail, and said, "I take it those are letters which can't be put off any longer."

She nodded.

Mason said, "Add this. Put it on top of the *'important'* pile."

"What is it?"

"A letter Paul Drake received."

"About that witness?"

"Yes."

"What does it say?"

"Read it."

Della Street took the letter, started skimming swiftly through it, then her eyes narrowed as she began to read more slowly and carefully. "Where's the key?" she asked at length.

Mason took it from his vest pocket.

Della Street looked at the key for a moment, then returned to the letter and read it entirely through once more.

"What do you make of it?" Mason asked.

"I don't know."

"A trap?"

"For whom?" she asked.

Mason said, "Now, there, Della, you've got me."

"If someone thought Drake would turn this letter over to you and that you would go there personally, I would say that it might be a trap for almost anything, but in view of the ad in the paper, the natural assumption would be that Paul Drake would send one of his men—just any one of his men."

Again Mason nodded.

"So," Della Street said, "if we rule out a trap, then what?"

"Could it have been written by the woman herself?" Mason asked.

"Why?"

"Perhaps an attempt to sell out the mysterious boy friend who didn't want to be recognized, and then get the hundred dollars for herself later on?"

"Now that could be," Della Street said.

"I wanted to get the feminine angle," Mason said.

She laughed. "There aren't any feminine angles, they're curves."

"Then this is a *fast* curve. What's your guess?"

"I don't like to stick my neck out, but I'd say your theory is the right one. It's a girl who wants a hundred dollars. She wants the Drake Detective Agency to discover the license number, find out it's the car that's wanted, and then she'll call for the reward. She'll do it all very surreptitiously so that the boy friend who was in the car with her doesn't know

9

she's furnished the tip. . . . Can you *prove* it's the car once you find it?"

"I think so," Mason said. "The car was going plenty fast. It shot in ahead of the Finchley Ford. Mrs. Finchley tried to stop, couldn't, and hit the hind end of this mysterious black sedan. Evidently the bumper on the black sedan hooked under her front bumper, swung her car completely around. She lost control and slammed into the lamppost, her twenty-two-year-old son was thrown out against the lamppost and smashed his hip."

"Then technically," Della Street said, "she ran into the black car instead of the black car running into her."

"That's what the driver of the black car will probably try to claim," Mason said, "but having speeded away from the scene of the accident, he'll hardly be in the position to make any defense that can't be torn to pieces."

"Can he say he didn't know he'd hit anything?"

"There must have been too much of an impact for him to get by with that. We can tell more when we see his car—if we ever do."

"What are you going to do about your mysterious Lucille Barton?"

"I'm going to go see her."

"Use the key and enter her apartment?" Della Street asked. "You'd better be sure you have witnesses and . . ."

Mason shook his head. "There's no reason to enter the apartment while she's away. If she's the witness we want, we can find out by talking with her. At least we *should* be able to."

"Between the hours of two and five?"

"Nope. That's when she'll be gone," Mason said, looking at his watch and grinning. "Between the hours of ten and eleven is the time I'm picking."

"Want a witness?"

"I don't think so, Della. I think I can do more by just dropping in and talking with her."

"Going to say anything about this letter?"

"No, I don't think so."

Della Street looked ruefully at the pile of important mail in the middle of Mason's blotter.

"You go ahead and answer it," Mason said, following her glance. "Figure out whatever needs to be done, and . . ."

"Chief, those are letters that simply must have your personal attention."

"I know," Mason said, "but think of Lucille Barton, probably sleeping late, the license number of the car that is responsible for Bob Finchley's broken hip in the upper right-hand pigeonhole of the desk in the living room . . . Sounds like rather an elaborate apartment for a working girl. What do you suppose Lucille Barton does?"

"Who said she worked?" Della asked.

Mason said to Della Street, "Make a copy of this letter, Della. I'm going to take a copy along with me and leave the original here. I may want to show her the letter but I see no reason for showing her the original."

Della Street nodded, moved over to her secretarial desk, ratcheted paper into the typewriter, and Mason watched while her skilled fingers flew over the keyboard.

Mason surveyed the finished results, said, "That looks a lot better than the original, Della."

"The original," she said. "was written by someone who had a hunt-and-peck system, but was awfully good at it, someone who had developed a lot of speed."

"That's the way I doped it out," Mason said.

"Probably on a portable typewriter."

Mason folded the copy of the letter Della Street had made, returned the key to his vest pocket, said, "I'm on my way."

"If you get arrested," Della Street observed smilingly,

"let me know and I'll be down with the checkbook and bail."

"Thanks."

"And if she isn't home," Della said, ceasing to smile, "please *don't use that key.*"

"Why not?"

"I don't know. There's something about it I don't like."

"There's a *lot* about it I don't like," Mason said. "What do you bet I don't walk in on a corpse, Della?"

"No takers."

"You keep that letter and the original envelope with the postmark in the safe," Mason told her. "I may have to square myself with the police."

"Meaning you're going to walk in if she isn't home?"

"Shucks," Mason said, grinning, "I never know just *what* I'm going to do."

Chapter 3

The address on South Gondola Avenue was a relatively small apartment house. The list of names on the left of the door indicated there were some thirty-five tenants.

Mason found without difficulty the name which had been clipped from the center of a visiting card, "Lucille Storla Barton." The figure opposite was "208" and there was a worn push button to the right and a speaking tube.

Mason deliberated for a few seconds over the push button, but curiosity about the key got the better of him. He fitted the key to the lock in the outer door and twisted it. The lock immediately clicked back and the door opened.

Mason found himself in a narrow lobby where a few uncomfortable chairs had been placed uninvitingly in a cold, symmetrical design. There was a public pay-station telephone in one corner and a cubbyhole office, separated by a low counter from the rest of the lobby. Back of this was a door marked "Manager" and on the counter was a placard reading, PRESS THIS BUTTON FOR THE MANAGER. Mason walked through the narrow lobby, into a corridor flanked with the doors of apartments. The elevator was lighted and back some thirty feet down the corridor. The building had three floors and Lucille Barton evidently lived on the second.

Mason pushed the button on the automatic elevator and when the lighted cage slid to a stop, opened the door, got in and pushed the button for the second floor.

Rattling upward, the lawyer realized it well might have been quicker had he climbed the stairs.

Apartment 208 was toward the rear of the building. Mason followed the doors back until he came to the one he wanted. He pressed a bell button and waited. There was no sound from within the apartment. Mason tried his knuckles on the door and again had no luck.

Surreptitiously, the lawyer inserted the key and twisted with thumb and forefinger.

The latch came smoothly back. The door opened.

Through the open crack in the door, Mason could look through a dark living room into a bedroom lighted by an overhead electric light. The bed had not been made and a feminine nightgown lay across it where it had been thrown. The lawyer could hear the sound of water running in a bathroom.

Mason gently closed the door, removed the key, waited in the corridor for some two minutes, then pressed the button again.

This time he heard sounds of motion and a feminine voice on the other side of the door asked, "What is it, please?"

"Is this Miss Barton?"

"Yes."

"I want to talk with you. My name is Mason. I'm a lawyer."

The door opened a cautious crack. He saw laughing, saucy blue eyes, wheat-colored hair, and a hand holding a robe tightly at the neck. Even, white teeth flashed in a smile. "I'm sorry, Mr. Mason," she said, "but I'm not presentable. I'm just getting up. You'll have to . . . to wait or come back."

"I'll wait," Mason said.

"I'm afraid I don't know you, Mr. Mason. I . . ." She looked him over from head to foot, then her eyes widened. "You're not *the* Perry Mason?"

"Perhaps you'd better say that I'm *a* Perry Mason."

She said, *"Honestly,* Mr. Mason!"

There was a moment of silence. Then she said, "Look,

Mr. Mason, it will only take me a second or two to get into some clothes. Things are in sort of a mess, but if you'll just step into the living room, please, and—you can raise the shades and make yourself comfortable—I'll be with you in just a few seconds."

"Or," Mason said, "I can come back, and . . ."

"No, no, come on in and sit down. It'll only take me a minute to make myself presentable."

She held the door open.

Mason entered the dark living room.

"If you don't mind raising the curtains, Mr. Mason, and—well, just sit down and make yourself at home."

"Thanks," Mason told her.

She moved swiftly across the sitting room to the bedroom and closed the door.

Mason walked over to the windows, raised the shades, and let in the morning sunlight.

Mason saw to his surprise that the apartment represented an incongruous clash of the cheap and the costly. A small but exquisite Oriental rug made the larger drab rug beside it seem hopelessly shoddy. The furniture was for the most part expensive, comfortable and had been selected with taste. Against this note of quiet luxury a few pieces of cheap furniture, their mediocrity emphasized by the aristocratic articles surrounding them, gave a jarring note.

On the table an ash tray was still well filled with cigarette stubs. Some of them had lipstick, some did not. A small kitchenette disclosed an empty bottle of Scotch on the sink, a couple of glasses, and two empty soda bottles. A magnificent, antique walnut writing desk was over in the corner. Mason hesitated for a moment, then swiftly walked over toward it, inserted his fingers in the ornamental metal handle on the top of the door and pulled. The desk was firmly locked.

Mason returned to a chair by the table in the center of the

room, picked up an old magazine, settled himself, crossed his legs and waited.

He had to wait about five minutes. Then the young woman came out of the bedroom wearing a chambray housedress which looked simple and domestic, but which had been carefully cut for the purpose of showing various curves and contours. She was wearing well-shaped shoes with medium high heels. Her legs were smoothly stockinged and very visible.

She said, "I'm not human in the morning until I've had my coffee, Mr. Mason. If you'll pardon me, I'll put a percolator on the stove. I suppose you've had breakfast."

"Oh, yes."

"You make me sound hopelessly lazy," she laughed, "but . . . how about a cup of coffee with me?"

"Thanks. Put my name in the pot and I'll join you."

She went into the kitchen, busied herself with the coffeepot.

"Nice apartment you have here," Mason said, getting up and strolling around the room.

"It's large," she said, "and I get the morning sun. The building is old-fashioned, but the way things are now that's very convenient. I have lots of elbow room and there's a private garage which goes with the apartment—and that's more than I'd have in a more modern apartment."

"I see you have a portable typewriter. Do you write?"

She laughed. "I pound out a letter once in a while. There *was* a time when I thought I was going to write the great American novel. I'm not only too dumb, I'm also too lazy."

Mason lifted the cover from the portable typewriter, said, "I want to make a memo. A matter has been bothering me. Would you mind if I used this typewriter for a minute? It's something that had escaped my mind until just now and . . ."

"Not at all," she said. "Go right ahead. There's some stationery in the drawer there in the table. I'll be with you in a minute. I'm going to put on some toast and a soft-boiled egg. How about you?"

"No, thanks. I've had breakfast. Just a cup of coffee for me, please."

Mason opened the drawer in the table. There were two piles of stationery, one the conventional full letter-size sheets such as are used in preparing manuscripts, the other a pink tinted stationery, apparently matching the stationery on which the letter that had been received by the Drake Detective Agency had been typed.

Mason fed a sheet of this paper into the machine and hurriedly wrote out a memo dealing with an imaginary witness in a fictitious case, involving the validity of a will, a witness who must be questioned along certain lines. When he had completed the memo, he put the cover back on the machine.

The aroma of coffee came from the kitchenette.

A few moments later Lucille Barton appeared with a tray and two coffee cups. There was toast on a plate, a small bottle of cream, a sugar bowl, a soft-boiled egg in a cup.

"Sure you won't have anything except coffee?"

"That's all, thanks," Mason said.

She put the tray on the table, said, "Just make yourself at home, Mr. Mason. I'm honored by this visit, but I'm also just a little bit frightened."

"Why frightened?"

She said, "I don't know. There's something about having a lawyer call on you, particularly a famous lawyer such as you are. I suppose—well, why suppose? Let me drink my coffee, and *then* tell me what it is."

She sipped her coffee, added cream and sugar, poured cream into Mason's coffee, and handed him the sugar bowl. After a few seconds she said, "Well, here's hoping it isn't too serious. What have I done, Mr. Mason?"

"Nothing as far as I know," Mason said. "That's delicious coffee."

"Thanks."

"Mind if I smoke?" Mason asked.

"Of course not."

Mason took his cigarette case from his pocket, lit a cigarette.

Lucille Barton munched on toast, watched him with speculative eyes, smiled easily and naturally whenever she caught him looking at her.

She was, Mason decided, in the late twenties, and evidently a young woman who knew her way around, but there was nothing hard about her. She seemed as naturally naïve and as spontaneous with her friendship as a young puppy, anxious to make friends with everyone in a joyful world.

"Well," she asked, "when do we start?"

"Now," Mason said. "Where were you on the afternoon of the third—day before yesterday?"

"Oh, good heavens," she said, and then laughed throatily.

"Where *were* you?"

"Is that a gag?" she asked, cocking a quizzical eyebrow. "Tell me, are you really serious?"

"Yes."

"The third—let me see. . . . Heavens, I can't tell you, Mr. Mason."

"Do you keep a diary?"

"Come, come, Mr. Mason. Do I look *that* dumb?"

Mason said, "I'll put it another way. Were you near the intersection of Hickman Avenue and Vermesillo Drive?"

She puckered her forehead in an attempt to search her recollection. "On the third?"

"On the third."

Slowly, she shook her head. "I don't believe I was."

Mason said, "Let's go at it again from a slightly different angle. I have reason to believe that you were with some man in a light-colored sedan. You had had a flat tire and had pulled into the curb to fix it. There was an accident there at the intersection just as you were getting ready to drive away, and you noticed something about the car, or about one of the cars that had been in the accident. It was a dark sedan and . . ."

She was shaking her head vigorously now. "Mr. Mason, I'm *quite* certain there's some mistake. At the moment I can't recall where I was, but I do know very definitely that I haven't seen any accident within the past few weeks and I certainly wasn't riding in any car which had a punctured tire. That's something a person wouldn't forget in a hurry, don't you think?"

"It would certainly seem so."

"I'm sure I wouldn't forget a thing like that. . . . Why are you interested, Mr. Mason?"

Mason said, "I'm representing the occupants of the car that was hit. There was a young man, Bob Finchley, a chap twenty-two years old, who has a broken hip. We hope it will heal up all right so he won't be crippled, but it's a serious injury, and it's certainly going to take some time, even with the best of luck, before he can . . ."

"Oh, that's too bad!" she interrupted. "I can't imagine anything worse than a young man being smashed up. I *do* hope there is no permanent trouble."

"We'll hope for the best," Mason agreed.

She finished the egg and toast, reached for a cigarette. Mason held a light and she placed her hands over his. She guided the match to the end of the cigarette. Her hands were warm, vital, and her touch was not too firm, not too delicate, just close enough to let the softness of her fingertips register for a moment on Mason's hand. Then, as she moved her own hand away, she slid the fingertips along the lawyer's fingers. "Thanks," she said, looking up at him with eyes that were suddenly serious. "I suppose you know, Mr. Mason, that I admire you tremendously."

"Do you?"

"I most certainly do. I've followed many of your cases. I think you're—well, you're brilliant and magnetic and powerful, and you're willing to stand up and fight for the underdog. I like that."

"Well, that's certainly gratifying," Mason said. "I try to do the best I can when I'm working on a case. Is there any way that you have of finding out where you were on the afternoon of the third?"

"Why, yes, Mr. Mason. I'm quite certain I can check back over daily events and puzzle it out. But I'm afraid I can't do it now. Having such a famous personage sharing coffee with me in my apartment is a little *too* much of a thrill. I don't suppose you know it but I'm as nervous as can be. This is something I'll remember for a long time, Mr. Mason."

"When do you suppose you can let me know where you were on the afternoon of the third?"

"I don't know. It may be—oh, it may come to me within an hour or two. Do you want me to telephone you?"

"If you will, please."

"I'll cudgel my wits—although it's very difficult for me to think back and remember just where I was on any given date. I mean even yesterday. Of course, if I keep thinking long enough, I'll remember some little thing and then that will pave the way for something else. Let's see . . . day before yesterday . . ."

"I take it you're not working at any regular job."

She smiled. "I have an allowance."

Mason impaled her eyes with his. "Alimony?"

She quickly averted her glance, then suddenly turned defiant eyes back to his. "Anything wrong with that?" she asked.

"Nothing," Mason said.

"And does it make any difference—in the matter you're investigating?"

20

Mason laughed, and said, "That would seem to be a nice way of asking me if it's any of my business."

"Well, I was just wondering what—well, whether you were investigating me and this story about the automobile accident was something to sort of pave the way."

"No," Mason said. "I'm telling you very frankly that I'm interested in you because I'm trying to uncover witnesses to that automobile accident."

"Well, I'm quite certain that I didn't see any automobile accident, and I'm quite certain that wherever I was on the afternoon of the third, I wasn't at the intersection of Hickman Avenue and—what was that other street?"

"Vermesillo Drive."

She said, "I know where Hickman Avenue is, but I don't even know where Vermesillo Drive is, Mr. Mason."

"You own a car?"

"Well, it's transportation. It's a good-looking car, but the engine is in bad shape."

"What color?"

"A light tan sedan."

"Well, of course," Mason interrupted, "that's primarily the point I'm interested in, but I *would* like to know just where you were at that time."

"How did you happen to come here in the first place, Mr. Mason?"

Mason smiled. "I can't divulge the source of my information, but I had reason to believe you might be the person I was looking for. You certainly answer the description."

"But you can't tell me how you got my description—who gave it to you?"

"No."

She said, "Mr. Mason, I wonder—do you believe in Fate?"

"Why not?" Mason asked with a swift glance of appraisal.

She said, "It just happens, Mr. Mason, that I'm in need of someone to—to do something for me—a lawyer."

Mason instantly became cautious. "I'm not in a position to take on any more responsibilities. I have a desk piled up with mail now and I . . ."

"But you took on this accident case and *that* only occurred day before yesterday."

"That's different. There was an element of urgency about it and, frankly, the case appealed to me."

She said, "Mr. Mason, let me tell you something about my case. I think *it* will appeal to you."

"I warn you, I can't handle it."

"Well, let me tell you anyway. I've been married twice. The first time was simply tragic. The last time I was—well, I was more cautious."

"And it worked out all right?" Mason asked.

"It didn't. My second husband was wealthy. That's one thing that helped. I had made up my mind I'd never marry again, but then he came along and he had money and—well, I married him."

"And the marriage broke up?"

"Yes, but I'm getting alimony."

"How much?"

"Two hundred dollars a week," she said.

Mason whistled.

"Well?" she asked defiantly. "Do you think that's too much? You should see how much money he makes!"

"I take it you weren't married very long."

"Five years, and during that time he made a lot of his money."

"That, of course, makes it different," Mason admitted.

"And now he's going into court trying to do something about my alimony, trying to get it reduced."

"You can't blame him for that."

"I thought perhaps you could talk to him and . . ."

Mason shook his head emphatically. "In the first place it

wouldn't be ethical for me even to talk to him. Your husband has a lawyer representing him and . . ."

"No, he doesn't, Mr. Mason."

"You mean he's taking the matter up with the Court by himself?"

"No, he . . . well, I'll explain it this way. He had a lawyer who made an application to have alimony reduced about six months ago and the Court refused to do it. The judge intimated he thought my husband had got slightly the best of the property settlement. You see, I worked with my husband in his business, and I really made a lot of that money for him. My husband got peeved at the lawyer he had and swears that when he takes the matter up in court again he'll do it himself."

"He'll probably wind up with some lawyer representing him, however," Mason said.

"I don't think so. Willard Allison Barton is a very determined, very ingenious individual. I think I'd be more afraid of him in a court than I would of any lawyer—except you, of course, Mr. Mason."

Mason said, "I don't do much work involving domestic relations."

"Mr. Mason, will you *please* listen?"

"All right," Mason said, settling back in his chair.

She said, "I'm going to marry again, and this time I *really* know it's going to work out all right. This man is an older man and a wiser man. He's very understanding. I feel differently about him than I have about the others."

"Well," Mason said, "that should dispose of the alimony matter. As soon as you get married again, your alimony will cease."

"But can't you see, Mr. Mason, I don't want to burn my bridges. I'm really entitled to this alimony. If you should warn Willard Barton that *you* were going to ask for an *increase* if he dragged me into court again, it would keep him from making a move."

23

"But if all alimony is going to cease within a few months, why not . . . ?"

She said bitterly, "I'm not going to let *him* off. I'd go to him and offer to settle the whole business for twenty-five thousand cash. He'd jump at that."

Mason said coldly, "And you want me to engineer that deal for you, is that it?"

She started balancing the spoon on the edge of the coffee cup.

"Well?" Mason asked.

She said, "You think I'm terribly scheming and designing. I'm only cautious. I want to protect my interests."

"So it would seem."

"Mr. Mason, look at it from a business viewpoint. Think of what a fool I'd be to give up two hundred dollars a week for any man, *any* man."

"If you were sure of having the alimony continue," Mason pointed out.

"Mr. Hollister wants to fix things so marrying him won't entail a financial sacrifice on my part. You *do* think I'm a golddigger, don't you, Mr. Mason?"

"You're certainly not madly in love."

"Well, Mr. Mason, it isn't as bad as it sounds. I've really been unfair to myself. As a matter of fact, it was Ross Hollister's own idea—I *did* tell him that I had finished with marriage, that I wasn't going to make any more matrimonial ventures, and then he asked me why and kept probing. You just have to see him to understand the sort of man he is. He's very understanding and sympathetic, but he's always probing. He has ways of working right into the back of your mind and pulling out ideas that you yourself hardly knew that you had."

"So he found out that you were worried about giving up two hundred dollars a week and a perfectly satisfactory alimony for a husband. Is that right?"

"That's right, and I'll tell you what he did, Mr. Mason,

all of his own accord. He put some property in trust so that it will be mine as soon as I marry him. He has already given me an insurance policy for twenty thousand dollars on his life and he's agreed to see that I have an allowance of seven hundred and fifty dollars a month just for my own clothes and spending money and things—you know, my own personal expenses, quite outside of running the household, and he has a very swank convertible roadster ordered that he's going to give me for my very own as a wedding present."

"Well," Mason asked, and then added dryly, "what more do you want?"

"I want his love and respect!" she blazed at him. "He's already made these arrangements. The papers have even been signed. The insurance has gone through—and if my husband comes into court and asks to have the alimony reduced, Ross Hollister will never *say* a word, but all of our married life he'll think I knew my financial boat was about to spring a leak and that I was looking for a transfer. *Can't* you see the thing from my position?"

"You're afraid that if your ex-husband starts a move to reduce the alimony Mr. Hollister will feel you knew that was coming, were afraid of the outcome and manipulated things so he . . ."

"Exactly!" she interrupted.

"When is your wedding going to take place?" Mason asked. "Why not hurry it up a little?"

She said, "Well, there's a little trouble about that. Mr. Hollister has been married before and there's some technicality—something about his divorce that's holding things up temporarily."

"I see," Mason said.

"Mr. Mason, can't you *please* go and talk with Willard Barton? He's at the Broadway Athletic Club. He lives there . . . but you mustn't give him any inkling, not even the faintest inkling as to the *name* of the man I'm going to marry.''

"Does he know Hollister?"

"Of course he knows him. Mr. Hollister is a member of the club, although he lives in Santa del Barra. Good heavens, Mr. Mason, they've even played poker together. Willard would die, just simply die, if he knew. In fact, you'll have to be very tactful in talking to him. He's inclined to be insanely jealous as far as I'm concerned—I guess that's one of the troubles—one of the reasons our marriage didn't work out better. He was always bringing my other husband into the conversation, wanting to know if I still didn't care for him, and . . .''

"Your first husband is alive?" Mason asked.

She went back to balancing the spoon on the cup.

"Is he?"

"Yes."

"And you have seen him recently?"

"Mr. Mason, *why* do you ask that question?"

"I don't know. I'm simply trying to get information."

"But I don't see why you . . .''

Abruptly Mason threw back his head and laughed, said, "You're a very ingenious young lady, Lucille. I have to give you a medal for ingenuity, but I'm not interested in your case, although I will admit that the unconventional approach intrigues me."

"What do you mean, the unconventional approach?"

Mason said, "You saw the ad in the paper. You evidently had some way of knowing that I was representing the Finchleys. You thought that if you could get me here and get me in a rather disadvantageous position, you . . .''

She pushed back the chair, her eyes were blazing. "Mr. Mason, that's absolutely uncalled for! That's entirely untrue. I don't even know what ad you're talking about! And there's certainly been no attempt to get you into what you are pleased to refer to as a 'disadvantageous position'! What do you think I am, anyway?"

"Well, what *are* you?" Mason asked.

"I'm a woman. I'm human and I've been disappointed in love. And I don't want to have my alimony reduced. I know you can scare my ex-husband to death. If he only thought I knew you, and that *you* were interested in me—in my case, I mean . . ."

Mason pushed back his chair, got to his feet, bowed and said, "I'm sorry, but I just don't believe you, and I can't waste any more time. It was a good attempt. I'm sorry that I can't fall for it. Perhaps if I had been *caught* in your apartment between two and five I might been forced to take your case. Thanks for the coffee."

Mason picked up his hat, walked to the door. "And that business of pretending you can't remember where you were day before yesterday is just a little too crude. Bait another trap and try another lawyer, Mrs. Barton."

And Mason pulled the door shut, leaving her standing there, her face flushed and angry.

Chapter 4

"Come on," Della Street said, "give."

Mason grinned. "A very nice girl with wheat-colored hair, laughing blue eyes, a luscious strawberry mouth with white, pearly teeth."

"Oh, my Lord," Della Street said. "He's in love."

Paul Drake said, "How old, Perry?"

"Somewhere between twenty-five and thirty."

Della Street brought a thesaurus and placed it on Mason's desk.

"Thank you, Della," Mason said. "Now let's see, Paul. How do I find exactly the words with which to describe her?"

Mason turned the pages, said, "Ah, yes, here we are, Paul—virtuous, maidenly, virginal, vestal, upright, moral, worthy, honorable . . ."

"What does she do for a living?" Drake asked.

"You would ask that," Mason told him.

"Come on," Della Street insisted, laughing, "let's have the story."

Mason walked over and sat on the corner of his desk, the left foot on the floor, the right foot swinging in an arc in mock embarrassment at their kidding.

"He's *afraid* to tell," Drake said.

"I do believe he's blushing," Della charged.

Mason said, "Well, if you want to know the truth, it *was* a trap."

"Badger game?" Drake asked.

"Don't be silly," Mason told him. "Apparently this girl

read the ad in the *Blade* and decided that while a detective agency was after the information, a lawyer must be in back of the detective agency."

"Go ahead," Drake said, "tell me about what happened when you opened the door."

"Apparently," Mason said, "she was in the bathtub."

"Oh, oh!" Drake observed.

"So," Mason said virtuously, "I noiselessly withdrew to the corridor, waited two minutes, then rang the bell. She let me in. You'd get a kick out of her apartment, a lot of perfectly grand furniture, which must have come from a settlement when her marriage broke up, mixed with some terrible junk which could have been part of the furniture in the place.

"There's an Oriental rug that's worth a lot of money. It's a beauty, and the desk is an antique that's in perfect condition. The ash tray and glasses show she was entertaining a man last night and didn't even bother to empty the ash tray when she went to bed—and they didn't break up the party until the Scotch was all gone.

"But she's clever. She seems almost naïve in her excessive friendliness, but back of it all she must be a scheming, cautious golddigger. She was *very* friendly. Having lured me into close quarters, she sized me up before planning the kill."

"What's the catch?" Drake asked.

"The catch," Mason said, "is that she wants some attorney to handle an alimony matter with her ex-husband. Having used the bait to lure me into the apartment, she proceeded to use her eyes, teeth, and her figure to hold my personal and undivided attention while she tried to interest me in a project to keep her ex-husband, one Willard Barton, who, I understand, is a rather practical, hardened, and exceedingly ingenious individual, from reducing her alimony to a figure materially less than the two hundred dollars a week which it costs her to live."

"Did she say anything about a retainer?" Della Street asked.

Mason grinned, and said, "Not a word."

"You're sure the thing was a plant?" Drake asked.

Mason said, "Judge for yourself."

He took from his pocket the sheet of pink stationery. "Here's some stationery that I mooched from the drawer in the table, Della. You might compare it with the stationery of the letter which we received. I also used the typewriter. We can check to see if this same machine was used in writing that letter."

Della Street hurried to the safe, brought out the original letter, held the two sheets of stationery side by side, and said, "The paper's the same."

"How about the typewriter?" Drake asked.

They bent over the desk studying the alignment of the type. "It's the same," Mason said. "Notice that 'g' is a little out of alignment, and the 'i' has dropped down a little and is canted over to the right."

"Well, that settles it," Drake said. "Hang it, I was hoping we had a lead. That hundred-dollar reward offer *should* get some action."

"Give it time," Mason said. "Remember the paper was hardly off the presses when this woman had her brain storm."

"Well," Della Street said, "since you have now spent most of the morning in a romantic adventure, I take it there'll be no objection on your part to tackling that pile of mail that's marked 'important.'"

Mason dismissed Drake with a gesture. "My nose, Paul, is being held to the grindstone. . . . Let me know if you get any answers to the ad."

Drake nodded.

When he had left the office, Mason and Della Street settled down to work. Coffee and sandwiches were brought in at noon, and by one-fifteen they had most the mail out of the way.

Gertie, the office receptionist, appeared with a letter. "A letter for you, Mr. Mason," she said. "It came by messenger. I thought you'd want to see it."

Mason groaned, "That, Della, is the reward of virtue. We try to get this pile of mail whittled down and what happens? More comes pouring in."

Della Street picked up a paper knife and slit the edge of the envelope, saying as she did so, "A plain envelope and—there's something in here, chief, something heavy."

"Probably another key," Mason said.

Della Street's voice showed surprise. "The paper that's in here, the stationery—chief, it's the same pink colored stationery, and it *is* another key."

She shook the envelope and a key fell out on the blotter. The key had an ornamental design at the end, was about two and a half inches long, hollow at the end of the shaft, with an intricate design of square-faced grooves on the part which was intended to actuate the lock.

"Looks like the key to a piece of furniture," Della Street said.

Mason, grinning, unfolded the letter. Della Street came to look over his shoulder.

Dear Mr. Mason:

I'm sorry that the desk was locked, so that you couldn't get the information you wanted this morning. I'm enclosing the key to that desk. The information you want is in a little leather notebook in the upper right-hand pigeonhole. You will find it on the next to the last page of the notebook—the license number of the car which collided with the Finchley automobile.

When it has been established quite to your satisfaction that this is the license number of the car you want, I will do something about collecting the hundred-dollar reward.

Very truly yours,
A FRIEND

Mason opened the drawer of his desk, reached for the magnifying glass, said, "Well, I suppose we may as well make a routine check of the typing."

Della Street's quick eyes caught the letters which were out of alignment.

"It's the same typewriter, chief," she said, "and the same stationery."

Mason nodded.

Della Street regarded Mason with brows that were knit together, causing two furrows in the otherwise smooth contours of her forehead. "Will you tell me what's the answer?"

Mason said, "I'm darned if I know. I have an uneasy feeling that I'm being played for a sucker."

"But surely, chief, she's smart enough, realizing you know it's a trap, not to expect you to walk into it a second time. And you simply can't expect her to be so dumb as to write this second letter on a typewriter that she knows by this time you have seen."

"Of course," Mason pointed out dubiously, "there are many people who don't realize that typing is as individual as handwriting. Not only does the type face tell the make and model of the typewriter on which a message is written, but the alignment gives a definite answer as to whether a document was or was not written upon a certain machine. However, it is surprising how many people fail to realize that."

"But, even so," Della Street pointed out, "that pink stationery. She *must* have known that you used some of it this morning."

"The thing gets me," Mason admitted, studying the letter.

Gertie, after a perfunctory knock on the door, pushed her head in and said, "A Lucille Barton is here, Mr. Mason. She said it would only take a minute and that she knew you'd want to see her."

Della Street smiled, "I'll have to have that thesaurus, chief. What were the words? Virginal, maidenly, sweet, attractive, charming, naïve . . ."

Mason grabbed up the letter and envelope, pushed them down into a drawer in his desk. He hastily dropped the ornamental key into the side pocket of his vest where it rubbed against the key to the apartment, said, "I'll see her, Gertie."

"There's a man with her."

"What's his name?"

"Mr. Arthur Colson."

Mason said, "Show them in, Gertie."

As Gertie nodded and closed the door, Mason turned to Della Street and said with swift decision, "Della, if I give you something to be typed for these people to sign before they leave the office, I want you to hold them here under one pretext or another. Be sure they don't get away."

"I don't get it," Della said.

"It will be a stall, Della. I want you to hold them so I can get down to her apartment and look in that desk."

"But, chief, isn't that just what . . ."

"I can't help it," Mason said. "My curiosity is aroused now. I'm going to find out what this is all about."

"But suppose she has . . ."

The door opened. Gertie, with an air of formality, said, "Miss Lucille Barton and Mr. Arthur Colson."

Lucille Barton came gliding across the office. Her tight dress emphasized her voluptuous figure, but the laughing candor of her eyes, the freshness of her face, and the spontaneous smile gave her an appearance of wholesome frankness.

"Mr. Mason, I couldn't understand the insinuations you made this morning. You thought I was lying about where I was on the afternoon of the third, trying to hold you up or something. And you mentioned an ad in the paper, so I read the ads, and found the one you must have been referring to.

So I decided to come and prove to you how wrong you were. Mr. Mason, I want you to meet Mr. Colson."

Arthur Colson, a slender individual, slightly stooped, with eyes that peered out studiously from under straight eyebrows, extended a thin, muscular hand with an air of preoccupation. "How do you do, Mr. Mason?" he said in a voice cultured almost to the point of affectation. "I suppose you wonder what I'm doing here. I do myself, but Lucille insisted. Impetuous as ever. Something about being a witness, I believe."

"Miss Street, my secretary," Mason introduced them. They both bowed.

"How do you do?" Della Street said.

"Will you be seated?" Mason asked.

Della Street picked up a pencil, held it poised over her notebook as she seated herself at her secretarial desk.

Lucille Barton went on hurriedly, "I feel that I owe this to you and to myself. You know, Mr. Mason, when I told you that I was no good at remembering what takes place from one day to another, I was fibbing a little. I was with Arthur on the third, but I wasn't certain he'd want to be—well—have his name mentioned. So I waited until I could get in touch with him and get his permission to tell you.

"You see I am working with Arthur. It's just a part time job, two to five. But the third was his day off, so we went to see *The Gay Prince*."

"A play?" Mason asked.

"A movie. It's a swell picture, Mr. Mason. One of those things that makes you feel sort of churned up inside."

Arthur Colson contented himself with a nod.

"Where was it showing?" Mason asked.

"At the Alhambra. It's a second-run picture, but we both missed it when it first came out and I've been wanting to see it. Arthur is terribly, terribly busy, but I've persuaded him to take one day a week off, even if he is working for himself. As I told him, 'All work and no play . . .'"

"Did you," Mason interrupted, "after leaving the theater, go to the vicinity of Hickman Avenue and Vermesillo Drive?"

Colson shook his head in positive negation.

"Heavens, no," Lucille said, laughing. "The Alhambra theater is way out at the other end of town, Mr. Mason. The show lasted until almost five o'clock and when we got out we . . ."

"Went to a cocktail lounge at a hotel near the theater," Colson observed.

The man had an almost dreamy air of abstraction, as though his mind, immersed in books, had somehow become imprisoned between the printed covers of some text book and had failed to emerge. With him, life might well be a series of dim experiences lived in a state of half-consciousness similar to that of a waking dream.

Lucille evidently noticed Mason's appraisal.

"Arthur's a chemist," she interpolated hastily and enthusiastically. "He's working on an invention of a new type of film that will react to infrared rays of light so that . . ."

Colson suddenly came to life. The absent-minded air of studious preoccupation dropped from him abruptly. He said sharply, "We won't discuss it now, Lucille."

"Oh, I just wanted Mr. Mason to know what you're doing, how successful you've been with inventions. And I wanted you to understand the relationship, Mr. Mason. I've invested a little money in financing him, and I work with him from two to five, doing his typing and things like that. Not that I'm too hot as a typist, but I can get by. And Arthur couldn't trust any regular stenographer with the things he's doing. He's so ingenious! This new invention is . . ."

"We haven't translated that invention into money yet," Colson warned. "It's better not to discuss these things."

Mason said, "I don't want to pry into your business, Mr. Colson, but I am interested in knowing what happened on the afternoon of the third. Now, as I understand it, you went to a cocktail lounge."

"That's right."

"And how long were you there?"

"Oh, I'd say an hour or so. We sat and drank cocktails and talked about the picture."

"And then we went to Murphy's for dinner," Lucille supplemented.

"And then?" Mason asked.

"Then we went home and—well, Arthur stopped up at the apartment for a drink or two—and we sat and talked some more."

"Until how late?" Mason asked.

They exchanged glances. Neither answered the question. Mason raised inquiring eyebrows.

Both suddenly answered the question at the same time.

"Eleven o'clock," Lucille Barton said positively.

"Half past twelve," Colson said, the two answers being almost simultaneous.

Lucille recovered her composure first. "What am I thinking about?" she said. "Of course, it was the week before that you had to leave early. It must have been just about half past twelve. . . . You see, Mr. Mason, Arthur takes one day a week off. The rest of the time he limits himself to a rigid schedule."

Mason said, "I'm very sorry to inconvenience you people, but this is very, very important. Would you mind dictating to my secretary a statement covering what you have just told me, and then wait until she's typed it, and after that affix your signatures?"

"But, Mr. Mason," Lucille Barton protested, "if we weren't there, what difference does it make if . . ."

"It's a matter of form," Mason interrupted. "Of course you don't have to do it. If you have any objection . . ."

"Not at all," Arthur Colson said. "We'll be glad to. In fact, Mr. Mason, there's a book I've been trying to get hold of, one which you probably have available here in your law library. I could be reading while your secretary is typing."

"What's the book?" Mason asked.

"Wellman, on the art of cross-examination."

"Indeed, yes," Mason said. "You may wait in the law library. How about you, Miss Barton?"

She surrendered reluctantly. "Very well, if Arthur wants to, I will. You might give me some of those magazines from the table in the outer office to look at while Arthur's reading. How long will it take?"

Mason said, "I suppose about half an hour. It should take you about ten minutes to dictate a complete statement, and then about twenty minutes for Miss Street to have it typed and ready for your signature. Now, if you'll excuse me, I have an appointment which I simply must keep. I'm very pleased I met you, and I'm certainly sorry if I am causing you any trouble."

"Not at all," Colson said. "There's something in that book I want to look up. I'll be very happy. After we've dictated the statement I take it that we may wait . . ."

"In the law library," Mason interrupted. "Della, you'll be as quick as you can, won't you?"

She caught and held his eyes. Her own eyes were apprehensive.

"Yes," she said.

Chapter 5

Mason stopped his car in front of the apartment house on South Gondola Avenue. A near-by cigar stand gave him access to a public phone.

Mason dropped a dime and dialed the number of his office.

He heard Gertie's voice saying, "Hello, Mr. Mason's office," and said, "This is Mr. Mason. Go into my private office, tell Della Street she's wanted for a moment and then put her on a phone where no one can hear her talk. Get it?"

"Just a minute," Gertie said. "I'll have you connected."

A moment later Mason heard Della Street's voice. "Okay," she said, keeping her voice low.

"How's everything coming?" Mason asked.

"Okay."

"Are they getting impatient?"

"Not particularly. How much more time do you need?"

"I'd say ten minutes," Mason said.

"I think I can safely promise you fifteen from here."

"Okay," Mason told her. "I just wanted to know the coast was clear."

"Be careful," she warned.

"I can't. I'm going to have to break an egg to make an omelet," Mason told her, and hung up.

He crossed the street, entered the apartment house, using the key he had received earlier in the day. This time he didn't bother with the elevator but climbed the stairs and walked rapidly to "208."

Mason took the precaution of sounding the buzzer some

two or three times to make certain there was no one in the apartment. Then he tried the key. The lock clicked back.

Mason entered the apartment and closed the door behind him.

The place had been made tidy. The ash trays had been cleaned and polished. The bed was made. Dishes had been cleaned up in the kitchen and the sink was spotlessly white.

Mason called out, "Hello. Anyone home?"

His voice echoed back from the empty apartment.

The lawyer took the desk key from his pocket, crossed to the desk and fitted the key to the lock. He twisted his wrist and the bolt clicked back.

Mason lowered the lid of the writing desk.

The interior was a miscellaneous assortment of confusion. There were letters lying about in the lower partitions. The upper pigeonholes were crammed with canceled checks, bank statements, more correspondence and memos.

The upper right-hand corner pigeonhole contained a small leather-covered notebook and a revolver.

Mason thumbed through the notebook. On the next to the last page on which there was writing, the lawyer found the figures of a license number, apparently hastily scrawled in pencil.

For the rest, the various notations were models of neatness—names, dates, telephone numbers, and mysterious figures evidently relating to some form of cash accounting in a code which Mason had neither the time nor the inclination to figure out.

Swiftly he copied the license number from the book, started to replace the book, then on impulse decided to take a look at the revolver.

Using a handkerchief over his fingertips so that he would leave no prints on the gun, Mason eased it out of the receptacle.

It was, he noted, a businesslike Smith and Wesson .38

caliber revolver. On the tang across the handle appeared the number "S65088."

Mason made a note of the number on the revolver, then replaced it, gently closed the desk, twisted the key in the lock, put the key back in his pocket and, using his handkerchief so that he would leave no fingerprints on the knob of the door, opened the apartment door.

The lawyer took the stairs two at a time, hurried across to his automobile, jumped in, and drove rapidly away.

He drove half a dozen blocks before he stopped in front of a drugstore, entered a telephone booth, dropped a coin and dialed his office.

"Hello, Gertie," he said, when he heard her voice on the line. "Get Della Street to come to the phone. Don't ring her telephone. Get her . . ."

"I understand," Gertie interrupted. "Just a minute."

A few moments later, Mason heard Della Street's anxious voice. "Hello, chief."

"Everything's okay," Mason said.

"Did you get it?"

"Yes. What's happening?"

"We still have five minutes to go at this end."

"It's okay. Get rid of them any time now."

"Okay."

"Be as casual as possible about it," Mason said.

"No trouble?" she asked.

"I'm not certain, Della, and I may have to revise my appraisal. She may want the hundred bucks but wants to make the chap with her feel she's on the up-and-up."

"You mean that he's her boy friend who . . ."

"I don't know," Mason said. "But whatever he is, I have a license number. It may be bait for a trap, in which event it's a more complicated trap than I thought. But if it should be the real thing, she'll be back sometime within the next day or two and want her hundred bucks. Don't worry, Della. Everything's okay."

Mason hung up and telephoned Paul Drake.

"Paul," he said, "I have a license number. I want the record of ownership on the automobile. Rush it through for me."

"What's the license number?" Drake asked.

Mason read the license number over the telephone, "9Y6370."

"Where are you now?"

"Hillcrest 67492," Mason said. "It's a pay station. I'll be sticking around. Make time on it, Paul, and call me back."

Mason had a coke at the counter, smoked a cigarette, then as the phone rang, he entered the phone booth.

Drake said, "It's a Stephen Argyle, living at 938 West Casino Boulevard—that's a swank neighborhood, Perry."

"Okay," Mason told him. "I'm going to gamble an hour's time."

"The car's a Buick sedan," Drake said. "No data on color. How did you get the license number, Perry?"

"That lead you had this morning. I can't talk about it now. Della can tell you all about it in ten or fifteen minutes. The parties are in my office now."

"Okay," Drake said. "I'll be sticking around. If there's anything you want, give me a ring. You have that address all right?"

"I have it," Mason said.

The lawyer left the drugstore, climbed into his car and drove out to the address on Casino Boulevard.

The house was a huge white stucco affair with red tile roof, porches, awnings, a well-kept lawn, hedges closely and neatly trimmed on each side, a driveway leading to a triple garage in the rear. A black Buick sedan was parked in the driveway.

Mason parked his own car at the curb, walked calmly up the driveway and began examining the Buick.

A fender on the rear had been straightened. There were a

few places on the rear of the body where it looked as though the paint had been skillfully matched and rubbed. The tire on the right rear wheel was brand-new.

Mason was looking at the rear bumper when the door opened. A man with broad shoulders, heavy square jaw and belligerent manner said, "What's the idea?"

Mason looked up and said without smiling, "Mr. Argyle?"

"No."

"Is he in?"

"What's that got to do with the way you're prowling around that car?"

"I'm not prowling. I'm examining it. Are you related to Mr. Argyle?"

"Not me. I work here."

"Indeed? What capacity?"

"Chauffeur and butler."

"In that event," Mason said, taking a cardcase from his pocket, "you may assume a more respectful attitude, take my card to Mr. Argyle, and tell him that I want to see him about a matter of the gravest importance—to him."

The chauffeur took the card, looked at it, said, "Very well," and started up the steps to the house.

Mason followed.

"Just a minute," the chauffeur said. "You wait here."

He went inside, closing the door behind him, reappeared after a few moments and said, "Yes, sir. You may come in."

The interior of the house was steeped in an atmosphere of quiet luxury. The aroma of an expensive cigar came from the room on the right. The chauffeur indicated this door, said, "In there. Mr. Argyle will see you."

The room was a combined den and library, with guns, books, comfortable leather chairs, hunting prints, photographs and an air of having been lived in. The portable bar in one corner was open, disclosing rows of bottles. A glass of Scotch and soda reposed on a smoking stand near the leather chair in which a man in the early fifties was seated.

He arose as Mason entered the room, said, "Mr. Mason, the lawyer?"

"That's right."

The man extended his hand. "I'm Stephen Argyle. I'm very glad to meet you. I have heard about you. Won't you sit down and join me in a drink?"

He was thin to the point of being bony, with long fingers, high cheekbones, bleached out eyes, thin hair which was well shot with gray. He wore glasses which clamped on the bridge of a high nose with a black ribbon hanging from the side, giving him an expression of austere power.

Mason said, "Thank you. I'll have a Scotch and soda, please."

Argyle nodded to the butler, who walked over to the portable bar, dropped ice cubes in a glass, mixed a Scotch and soda, wordlessly handed it to Mason.

"Nice room you have here," Mason said. "It's comfortable, has the feeling of being lived in."

"I spend much of my time here. Would you care for a cigar?"

"I'll have one of my cigarettes, if you don't mind." Mason opened his cigarette case.

As he tapped the cigarette on the side of the cigarette case, he saw that the butler and chauffeur had no intention of leaving.

"You'll pardon me," Mason said, striking a match, "if I'm rather abrupt. My time is somewhat limited."

He lit the cigarette, blew out the match and dropped it in an ash tray.

"Go right ahead," Argyle said.

Mason glanced at the chauffeur who was standing by the bar.

Argyle made no move to dismiss the man.

"On the afternoon of the third of this month," Mason said, with complete assurance, "at about five o'clock, your Buick out there was involved in an accident at the intersection of Hickman Avenue and Vermesillo Drive. Who was driving it, you or your chauffeur?"

"That's a question?" Argyle asked, raising his eyebrows.

"A question about who was driving it," Mason said. "The part about the accident isn't a question. It's an assertion."

"Really, Mr. Mason, I'm surprised! Surprised beyond words."

"I take it, then, *you* weren't driving it?"

Argyle hesitated for a minute, then said, "No."

Mason glanced at the chauffeur, whose eyes had suddenly become as intent as those of a cat stalking a bird.

"As a matter of fact," Argyle said, carefully weighing his words, "you are bringing information which confirms my worst fears. I trust the accident was not serious."

"It was serious," Mason said. "What about your fears?"

"My car was stolen on the afternoon of the third. The police recovered it later on that evening, parked in front of a fireplug in the downtown district. The gasoline tank was half empty and the car had been driven over a hundred miles."

"Quick work," Mason said.

"On the part of the police?" Argyle asked.

Mason smiled.

Argyle frowned.

Mason said, "I'm representing Bob Finchley. His mother was driving the car. She was badly shaken up. The car was pretty well wrecked. Bob Finchley sustained a broken hip. It's too early yet to tell whether there will be complications."

"Indeed. That's too bad," Argyle said. "I will have to consult my lawyers. As I understand it, Mr. Mason, in the event I let anyone use my car *with my permission* I am responsible for damages, but, of course, in the event of theft . . ."

Argyle shrugged his shoulders, tapped ash from the end of his cigar.

Mason said, "Let's quit beating around the bush. That stall about the stolen car is two years older than Moses. In addition to which, it stinks."

The chauffeur took a step forward.

Argyle waved him back.

"Now, Mr. Mason," Argyle said, "I'm satisfied that as an attorney you wouldn't want to make any insinuations."

"All right," Mason said, "I'll go at it the long way round. *When* was the car stolen?"

"Sometime around three o'clock in the afternoon."

Mason smiled. "When was the car *reported* stolen?"

"I didn't miss it until around seven o'clock," Argyle said. "I had left it parked at the curb in front of my club. I went out to get in the car and it was gone."

"And you immediately reported it to the police?"

"Yes, sir."

"Using the club telephone?"

"Yes, sir."

"And how far away from the place where the car was stolen was it recovered?"

"I would say not over eight or ten blocks."

Mason said, "The boy's pretty badly injured. He's going to be laid up for a while and the mother has of course suffered nervous shock. Then there's the matter of the car."

"Surely, Mr. Mason, you don't think I'm liable."

"Why not?"

"I tell you the war was stolen."

Mason grinned. "As you so aptly stated, as a lawyer, I'm too smart to make any accusations—in front of witnesses. You'll have a lot of fun listening to what I tell a jury, however."

"*Surely*, Mr. Mason, you don't doubt my word. Good

heavens, I'm a responsible citizen! My car is fully insured. If there were any question of liability on my part, I would be only too glad to make an adjustment. As it is, my insurance company will handle things."

"All right," Mason said. "If that's the way you want it, I'll do business with your insurance company."

"Provided, of course, there's any liability."

"Oh, certainly," Mason said. "What's the name of the club where you spent the afternoon?"

"The Broadway Athletic Club."

Mason got to his feet. "Nice to have met you," he said, and started for the door.

Argyle arose, hesitated, then sat down again.

The chauffeur saw Mason to the door.

"Good afternoon, sir," he said.

A moment later the door slammed.

Chapter 6

The office of the Drake Detective Agency was on the same floor as Mason's offices. Mason stopped in hurriedly for a few words with Paul Drake.

"By gosh, Perry, we hit the jack pot. I can't figure out how it happened, but it's the jack pot!"

"I want men on the job immediately, Paul. Men who can really do an intelligent job. I want Stephen Argyle checked for the afternoon of the third. He was probably at the Broadway Athletic Club. I want to know how much he drank. I want to know how long he was there. I want to know whether people who were there with him noticed any break in the continuity of his visit. I want to find out everything we can from the doorman. I think the doorman may have been bribed. I don't think we have enough money to compete with Stephen Argyle, on bribery, so we're going to have to throw a scare into the doorman. I want a man who can *really* scare the guy.

"I want to find out all about the records of Argyle's car, which was supposed to have been stolen on the afternoon of the third, when it was reported stolen, when it was recovered, all about it. I particularly want to find out if Stephen Argyle didn't drive up to the Broadway Athletic Club in a taxicab sometime between five and six. At that hour people were dropping in for cocktails and you should be able to find some club member who saw him arrive in a taxi. You're going to have to work fast."

"Okay," Drake said, "I'm on the job. How many men shall I put out?"

"As many as it takes," Mason said. "We're going to get the dope and when we get it, we're going to send the bill to Stephen Argyle and make him pay it and like it."

"He's the man all right?"

"It was his car," Mason said, "and I think he's the man. Incidentally, I want to find out everything I can about him. I have an idea his wife is dead or has recently left him."

"What gives you that idea?"

"He has a butler and chauffeur," Mason said, "who certainly wouldn't get along for five minutes in a house where there was a woman. Yet the house on Casino Boulevard is a great big place and apparently Stephen Argyle does most of his living in one room, a room which fairly reeks of tobacco."

Drake said, "Okay, Perry, I'll put men on the job right away. By the way, Perry, you were right about that flirtatious young grass widow. She sent her little playmate in to collect the hundred bucks."

"Well, she's entitled to it. Hang it, I can't figure that one out. She certainly had me fooled. When did this dame come in for the reward?"

"Not over five minutes ago," Drake said. "I sent her down to your office and told her Della Street, your secretary, would take care of it."

"Who is she?" Mason asked.

"A right cute number, name of Carlotta Boone. She was very coy about it and, of course, wouldn't let on that she knew anything at all about Lucille Barton. She simply said she'd come to collect the hundred dollars reward."

"I'll go see her," Mason said. "You rush men out to get the dope on Argyle. I'm *really* going to shake him down for a settlement—we'll give that Finchley kid a chance to finish his college education in return for the inconvenience of a broken hip."

"Don't let Argyle off the hook too easy," Drake warned. "I detest these hit-and-run boys who try to get away with it,

48

and who probably have enough political pull to help them out in case the going gets tough."

"I'll stick him," Mason grinned. "And now I'll go pay Lucille her hundred dollars. It's going to be interesting to listen to the way Carlotta Boone tries to get the hundred without betraying Lucille's frame-up. Okay, Paul, I'm on my way."

Drake said, "I'll have men on the job within five minutes."

Mason walked down the corridor to his own office, whistling a little tune. He unlocked the door of his private office, entered, grinned at Della Street, sailed his hat over to the shelf in the coat closet and said, "Well, Della, I understand Lucille has sent a stooge for the hundred dollars."

Della Street's face was a mask of perplexity. "Wait until you hear *her* story."

"I want to," Mason grinned. "Is it good?"

"I haven't had time to get all of it," Della Street said, "but it's one that's going to knock you for a loop."

"What's the name again?" Mason asked.

"Carlotta Boone."

"What sort, Della?"

"Brunette, slender, shrewdly calculating, probably a golddigger, reticent about herself. She resents me, wants to talk with you, says she came to give information and get a hundred dollars, and doesn't want a run-around."

Mason grinned, said, "Well, let's get her in, Della, listen to her story, give her the hundred bucks, and send Lucille's keys back. Maybe this kid shares the apartment with Lucille. Anyway, bring her in."

Della Street said, "Just don't jump to conclusions, chief. The talk I've had with her indicates it may be something entirely different."

"Oh well, get her in," Mason said, "and we'll find out what it's all about."

Della Street picked up the telephone, said, "Send Carlotta Boone in, Gertie."

Then Della went to the door of the private office to open it and usher the visitor across the threshold.

She had black, lacquered eyes which were for the most part utterly devoid of expression but glistened with vigilance. Her hair was a deep glossy black. She was about two inches taller than the average woman and about ten pounds lighter, and there was a peculiar, wary tension about her.

"Well, how do you do, Miss Boone?" Mason said. "I understand you came to collect a hundred dollars."

"That's right."

"How did you happen to get the information?" Mason asked. "How did you know so much about where the number was written down?" He winked at Della Street.

"You mean the license number?"

"Yes."

"Because I'm the one who wrote it down."

"Oh, I see," Mason said. "And then you placed it in the desk?"

"I placed it in my purse," she said. "How do we fix it up about paying the hundred dollars? Of course, I understand that you can't afford simply to dish out a hundred bucks to every girl who comes in here with a plausible story and a license number."

Mason, grinning amiably, said, "Certainly not. However, I think we've pretty well established our point in the present case."

Della Street coughed warningly.

Mason glanced at her, frowned, then became cautiously on guard.

Carlotta Boone settled herself in the chair, took pains to cross her legs so that she showed a good expanse of stocking. Her legs, while thin, were well streamlined.

She said, "I suppose I can trust you."

"I suppose you'll have to," Mason said.

She had started to reach into her purse. Now she stopped and regarded Mason with an appraisal that indicated her inherent suspicion. "How do *I* know you're not going to double-cross me?"

Mason said, "After all, young lady, *I've* been in business some time. And before I pay you the money I want all the details of the story."

"Oh, all right," she said wearily, "here's your number."

She pulled a slip of paper from her purse and handed it to Mason.

Mason glanced at the number, then frowned, looked at it again and said, "I'm sorry, Miss Boone, but I think it's only fair to tell you in advance that this is the wrong license number."

"How do you know?"

"Because I already have the information I wanted. I have not only the license number of the automobile, but I have inspected the automobile, and have talked to the owner. Quite obviously this is the wrong number."

"It's not the wrong number," she said with firm determination. "What are you trying to do? Talk me out of the hundred dollars? Don't think I'm *that* easy."

Mason frowned.

She said angrily and defiantly, "I was with my boyfriend. We'd been out for a rendezvous at one of the cocktail bars. We'd done a little dancing. He was driving me home. We had a flat tire. I got out and was standing around looking ornamental and giving a little help here and there. He got the tire changed. We were just finishing with it, when there was a terrific crash at the intersection. I saw this big black sedan roaring and swerving down Vermesillo Drive. Behind it there was a Ford coupe that was skidding all over the road. It smashed into a telephone post just as I looked up. A woman and a man were in it. The man seemed to be pinned between the door and the post. The woman who was driving had bumped her head. I thought there

51

might be an opportunity for—well, frankly, Mr. Mason, I thought I could make some money. I saw the big black car was going to make a run for it. I pulled out my notebook and jotted down the license number. All right, I didn't give it to the police. I waited for a reward to be offered. I kept looking at the ads."

Mason, frowning, regarded her.

"And why not?" she went on defiantly. "You'll get plenty out of this case. You aren't working for nothing. Why should I? I need money a lot more than you do, Mr. Perry Mason!"

Mason turned to Della Street. "Get Drake on the phone," he said.

A moment later, when Paul Drake was on the phone, Mason said wearily, "Paul, here's another license number for you—49X176."

"What about it?" Drake asked.

Mason said, "Find out who owns the car, the address and the type of car."

Mason hung up the phone, said to Carlotta Boone, "This is a new development. It's an unexpected development. I thought we had the license number we wanted."

"I can readily understand," she said, "that with an ad such as you have placed in the paper you must have been deluged with girls who were willing to tell a good story and give a license number in return for a hundred dollars. However, I'm giving you the straight goods. The question is, do you want it or don't you?"

"What do you mean by that?"

She said, "You're not kidding me. The man who was driving that sedan is in a jam. He's mixed up in a hit-and-run case. If I wanted to, I could go to him and shake him down for ten times what I can get out of you."

"Why don't you do it, then?"

"Because it's too risky. It's blackmail. You could do it as a lawyer. I can't."

"So what do you want?"

She said, "I put myself in your hands. I want you to investigate that license number. When you're convinced that that's the car, you can give me the hundred dollars."

"All right," Mason said. "What's your address? How do I get in touch with you?"

"You can't, and you don't," she said. "*I'll* get in touch with *you*, and of course I don't want my name mentioned. The boyfriend I was with is married. He'd have a fit if he knew I had come to you. But, after all, a girl has to live!"

"And when will you get in touch with me?" Mason asked.

"Sometime before noon tomorrow. You should know by then. Good night."

With complete assurance, she arose from the chair, marched to the exit door, jerked it open and walked out.

Mason looked at Della Street, scratched his head, and said, "If you'd like to go in for a slight understatement, Della, this is what might be called a complicating factor."

"You don't suppose that that's some ruse this man has worked out to throw you off the trail, do you?" she asked.

"Probably," Mason said, "but it's not going to throw me off the trail. I'll now go out and chase after the red herring, but Paul Drake is going to keep after the real quarry."

The telephone rang. Drake said, "Your man is Daniel Caffee. The car's a Packard sedan; the address is 1017 Beachnut Street. What about him?"

Mason said, "You getting your men on the Argyle job?"

"They're on. Four men are out right now, and two more are on their way."

Mason nodded to Della Street, said, "Get your hat and a notebook, Della. We'll leave Paul here to handle this end of the business. You and I are going to chase a red herring."

Into the phone he said, "That's fine, Paul, you stay on the job. I'm going out to take a look at Mr. Daniel Caffee."

"Okay, Perry, I'll get all the dope on Argyle. However,

he'll know that we're investigating him. I can't have my men contact these club members without some of them getting in touch with Argyle and telling him what's going on."

"That's all right," Mason said. "That's the way I want it. Let's let him know we're on the job."

Mason hung up the phone, said, "Come on, Della, let's go."

Chapter 7

Driving along Beachnut Street, Della Street said, "Why do you suppose a girl would pull a trick like that?"

"Probably to get a hundred bucks," Mason said. "But, hang it, Della, there's something about that girl which impresses me."

"She's a golddigger."

"I know she's a golddigger. She took down the license number, intending to use it for blackmail. Then for some reason she didn't. She saw the ad in the paper offering a hundred dollars. She couldn't resist the temptation of cleaning up a hundred dollars where her action would be entirely within the law. Somehow or other the girl gives me the impression of telling the truth, and yet—well, hang it, Della, I've already seen Argyle's automobile. It has dents on the back end; it's been in a collision, the right rear wheel is brand-new, and . . ."

"And, of course," Della Street said, "his story about the car having been stolen *could* have been true."

"Just about one chance in a hundred, Della. Well, we'll soon find out. Here's 1017."

Mason brought his car to a stop in front of a goodlooking apartment house, quite obviously of the better class.

"What do we do?" Della Street asked. "Barge on in?"

"No," Mason told her. "We look around a bit first. There's a private garage down here in the basement. There'll be someone in charge. Let's park the car and take a look."

Mason found a parking place for his car, then he and

Della Street walked down the sharply inclined ramp to the garage.

The man in charge was parking cars.

Mason looked around the place, said to his secretary, "Keep looking for a big black Packard, Della. You take the left side, I'll take the right. Let's go."

The man finished parking the car, called out, "Hey, you!"

Mason turned and waved his hand reassuringly.

Della said, "Here's a Packard over here on the left."

Mason took a quick look at the license number, said, "That's the one, Della. Okay, let's give it a once-over."

The man who ran the garage was walking toward them now. "What do you folks want?" he called.

Mason, moving toward the rear of the Packard, said, "You talk with him, Della. Tell him we understand the car is for sale."

The light was dim there in the back of the garage, but Mason could see that a new fender assembly had been put on the back of the car, that there was still a dent in the trunk and that the left rear tire bore marks of a deep gouge.

Mason heard Della Street explain that they understood the car was for sale and then heard the garage man insisting that they'd have to talk with Mr. Caffee about it.

Mason completed his hurried inspection, handed the garage man ten dollars and said, "Mr. Caffee is the one who offered the car to a friend of mine. I wanted to get the low-down on it."

"Yes, sir," the garage attendant said, instantly mollified.

"Now, as I understand it," Mason said, "the car was in some sort of a wreck."

"Oh no, sir, not a wreck. The car's in wonderful shape. Just a minor traffic collision that made it necessary to put on a new fender. That is, the old fender *could* have been fixed up but Mr. Caffee's very particular about the car, keeps it running like a watch."

"I see," Mason said. "When was this accident?"

"Oh, not very long ago—a couple of days. Mr. Caffee just got the car back. He has some sort of a pull with the car agency here. I don't think the agency did the installation for him, though. I know he got the fender through them. Anyhow the car wasn't hurt a bit. It was just a little sideswipe. The rear bumper got most of the damage. It was torn loose from its supports, but that's all been fixed up now."

"I see," Mason said. "Well, thanks a lot. I suppose Caffee is in now?"

"Oh yes, sir. Sure. When his car's here, he's here. He always drives when he goes out."

"Married?"

"Yes. His wife has her own little coupe. She doesn't like the big car. Mr. Caffee says he likes weight and power and speed—he's that sort."

"I see," Mason said. "What's the number of his apartment, by the way?"

"22-B."

"Could you describe him to me?" Mason asked. "I always like to know the sort of chap I'm doing business with."

"Why yes, sir. He's—oh, I should say he was around fifty-five, rather slender, a quiet sort of man who always dresses in good taste, smokes cigars, wears double-breasted gray suits, nearly always gray. I don't think I've ever seen him in any other color."

"Okay, thanks," Mason said. "We'll go see him. The car looks to me like a pretty good buy."

"I didn't have any idea he intended to sell it. He's only had it a few months, and I know he likes it very much."

"Can we take an elevator here?"

"Yes, sir. You can ring and the elevator comes right down here. As visitors, you're supposed, of course, to stop by the desk and be announced."

"I know," Mason said, "but that's a useless formality, under the circumstances. What floor is Apartment 22-B on?"

"The fifth floor."

Mason said to Della Street, "Come on, Della. We'll at least make Mr. Caffee an offer."

The garage attendant pushed the buzzer which brought the elevator down to the basement.

Mason closed the door, punched the button for the fifth floor.

"Well?" Della Street asked.

Mason shook his head. "I'm going around in circles. This whole business is completely cockeyed."

The elevator lurched to a stop at the fifth floor.

Mason pushed a mother-of-pearl button by the side of the door numbered 22-B, and within a few seconds the door was opened by a man with thin gray hair who was in the late fifties. He was attired in a double-breasted gray suit and was smoking a cigar.

"Mr. Caffee?" Mason asked.

"Yes, sir."

Mason shoved a card at Caffee, said, "I'm Perry Mason, the lawyer. I want to talk with you about your automobile."

"What about it?"

Mason pushed forward.

Caffee instinctively fell back. Mason and Della Street walked into the apartment.

"What about my automobile?" Caffee asked.

"I want to know about the accident you had on the third."

Caffee stood rigid for a moment, then his lip began to quiver, the cigar almost fell from his mouth. Caffee clutched at it hurriedly, cleared his throat, said, "What do you mean?"

"You know what I mean," Mason charged, his manner radiating positive assurance. "Your automobile smashed into a Ford coupe at the intersection of Hickman Avenue and Vermesillo Drive. I suppose you'd had a few drinks, were afraid to stay and take the rap, and decided you could escape undetected. A look in the rearview mirror showed you that all eyes were focused on the car that was crashing into the lamppost. You were going fast and you kept on going fast."

"Oh, my God!" Caffee exclaimed, and collapsed into a chair. His face seemed suddenly to be made of bread dough. His lips trembled.

"Well?" Mason demanded.

"You've got me," Caffee said pathetically. "Why in the world did I ever do it?"

Della Street dropped into a chair, opened a shorthand book, balanced it on her knee, and started taking notes.

"You admit it?" Mason asked.

"Yes," Caffee said, "I admit it. You've caught me. You've caught me dead to rights. I supposed at the time there was just property damage. . . . Tell me . . . was anyone hurt, Mr. Mason?"

"Two people were hurt," Mason said. "The woman who was driving the car was shaken up. The son sustained a broken hip. He was slammed against the lamppost when the door of the car jerked itself open and spilled him out. It's a wonder he didn't crack his head and die."

Daniel Caffee put long, bony hands to his head, moaned.

"Well," Mason said, "what about it?"

"You've caught me," Caffee repeated in abject contrition. "I suppose I'll have to take my medicine. Mr. Mason, I give you my word, I didn't know anyone had been hurt. I kept hoping it was just a question of property damage and I was trying to find some way of paying off . . . I was a coward. I'd had a few drinks too many. You see, I'd met an old friend and we'd stopped in a cocktail lounge. Ordinarily I never drink if I'm going to drive. My wife was expecting me and I—well, I was late and I was trying to make time. I was going fast. I hit that intersection and honestly I didn't see the other car until it was right on top of me. I thought I could give my car the gun and get by. I pushed the throttle down to the floor boards. My car has a marvelous pickup. It shot ahead and all but missed that other car, but that other car couldn't seem to stop. It seemed to me to keep right on coming. It hit the rear end of my car and I guess my rear bumper snagged the front wheel and jerked the other car around and into the ornamental lighting pole.

"At first I thought I'd stop. Then I looked in the rearview mirror and, just as you say, I saw that everyone was running toward the other car. The street was clear ahead, and I new that there were no traffic signals for half a dozen blocks, so I just kept the car rolling. I felt sure that no one had seen me well enough to recognize the car, and my car had suffered relatively little damage. If it hadn't been for those drinks I'd never have even considered any such crazy idea."

"What time was this?" Mason asked.

"I guess it must have been shortly after five o'clock, Mr. Mason."

"Where?"

"Right there at the intersection of Hickman Avenue and Vermesillo Drive. I was traveling east on Vermesillo Drive and, as I say, I was hurrying right along."

Mason glanced at Della Street's busy pen.

"And the date?"

"The third of the month. Mr. Mason, I know that I'm in bad, but let's do what we can to square it. I'm covered by insurance. I'll get in touch with the insurance company and I know that they'll make a generous settlement. In addition to that, I'll make your clients a check for ten thousand dollars on my personal account. I suppose technically I'm guilty of hit-and-run and I'll have to take my medicine there. And I *do* hope we can handle this without my wife finding out about it."

"Your wife's home now?"

"No, I'm expecting her in about thirty minutes."

Mason narrowed his eyes, thinking the situation over.

He said, "Write out a brief statement of what you've just told me. Sign it and make a check for ten thousand dollars, payable to Robert L. Finchley.

"The hit-and-run angle you'll have to handle with the police. I suppose under the circumstances, and in view of the payment, you may get probation. Now, while you're writing out that statement and the check, do you have a telephone I can use?"

"Yes, sir, right over there on the table."

Mason walked over to the telephone, asked for an outside line, gave the number of Drake's office.

When he had Drake on the phone he said, "Paul, that Argyle thing was a false alarm. Call off your men."

"The hell it's a false alarm," Drake said indignantly. "One of my men has a signed statement from the doorman at the Broadway Athletic Club. He says Argyle showed up in a taxicab about seven o'clock. He seemed all upset and nervous. He told the doorman he was going to report his car as having been stolen, and gave the guy a hundred bucks to swear Argyle had been there ever since noon. The doorman would have stayed put if my man hadn't pulled everything in the quiver and told the guy he was going to the pen for compounding a felony."

Mason remained silent.

"You there?" Drake asked.

"I'm here."

"Argyle's wife left him about six months ago. He's a speculator in oil leases. He has two associates, Dudley Gates and Ross P. Hollister. Hollister lives in Santa del Barra and has the dough. Since Argyle's wife left him Argyle has been living alone in his big house, only the chauffeur with him and a maid who comes in by the day. Argyle is well thought of at the club. He's considered to have made a nice nest egg in that new oil field up north.

He'd been drinking and was still a little woozy when he slipped the doorman at the club the hundred bucks. Now what more do you want than that, Perry? He's your man."

"He *can't* be!"

"I take it you're where you can't talk without someone hearing you?"

"That's right."

"Well, don't let him flimflam you, whoever he may be," Drake said. "He's giving you a run-around. Argyle's the man you want."

"He's giving me a written confession and his personal check for ten thousand bucks," Mason said in a low voice, and hung up the telephone just as he heard Paul Drake's gasp of astonishment.

Chapter 8

Mason, driving his car rapidly along Beachnut Street, said to Della Street, "All right, Della, I'm going to take you down to the Ketterling Hotel. You'll be able to get a taxi there. Go see Paul Drake, tell him about these new developments, then go to my office and wait for me to call you.

"I'm going back to talk with Argyle, then I'm going to that South Gondola Avenue address."

"You be careful. I think that whole thing is a trap."

"I know," Mason said, "but someone is playing games and I want to find out who."

Mason drove rapidly and in silence to the Ketterling Hotel.

Della said, "Now, as I understand it, I'm to call on Paul Drake, fill him in with what's happened, and then go to the office and wait?"

"Right."

"I'll be there," she told him, jumping out of the car. "Good luck to you."

He grinned. "That's the trouble, we're shot with luck. We have two guilty drivers and only one smashup."

He drove to Argyle's house at 938 West Casino Boulevard. The big Buick was no longer in the driveway. Nor did Mason get any answer when he rang the bell on the front door.

He returned to his car and, driving more rapidly now, went at once to South Gondola Avenue, where he took the precaution of parking his car a couple of blocks from

Lucille Barton's address. Then, having walked to the apartment house, he circled around to the rear, to inspect the garages.

Without much difficulty he found the garage bearing the number "208." The doors were closed, but not locked. The interior was dark and gloomy.

Mason opened the door far enough to enable him to see that there was no automobile in the garage.

Having satisfied himself on that point, Mason crossed the street and walked down to the corner to a cigar store where there was a public telephone.

Dialing the unlisted number of his private office, he waited until he heard Della Street's voice.

"Hello, Della," he said in a low voice. "I've looked the place over. She's out somewhere in her car. I'm going to try and find that notebook."

"I was afraid you'd do something like that. How long will you be?"

"Not long."

She lowered her voice and said, "Mr. Argyle's in the waiting room. He's having kittens."

"What's happening?"

"Apparently his conscience is bothering him."

"You don't think he wants to retract any of the statements he made?"

"Apparently not."

"How long has he been there?"

"He says he left his place immediately after you talked with him. He's really worred about something. He tells me he couldn't talk freely with you when you were there and he's very anxious to see you now."

"Why couldn't he talk freely?"

"He didn't say."

"There's only one reason I can think of, his chauffeur and butler was present."

"Well, why didn't he simply send the man out?"

64

"I don't know. There's something strange about that relationship."

Della said, "The chauffeur was down there sitting at the wheel of the Buick when I came in. Mr. Argyle went down right afterwards to tell him he needn't wait. That was when I told him I didn't know when you'd be in. Argyle says he's going to wait, no matter how long it is."

"Okay," Mason said. "I'm on my way, Della. Try and hold Argyle there."

Mason hung up the phone, walked rapidly up the street to the entrance of the apartment house, used his key to open the outer door, ran up the stairs to the second floor, made certain that the second floor corridor was empty, and then walked rapidly back to Apartment 208.

Mason knocked, and received no answer.

He made another quick survey of the corridor, then quietly inserted his key in the door, clicked back the lock and, opening the door, stepped swiftly inside the apartment.

Lights were on in the apartment. The desk was open. The upper right-hand pigeon hole was empty. Both the notebook and the gun had disappeared.

Mason gave an exclamation of annoyance, took two steps toward the bedroom, then stopped.

From where he was then standing, he could look through the half-open bedroom door, across the lighted bedroom and through an open door into a bathroom.

A girl was standing in the bathtub behind a shower curtain, and evidently had just shut off the water.

A white enameled bathroom stool was standing beside the bathtub. On this stool was a blued-steel revolver, squat, ominous and ugly.

As Mason stood watching the silhouette of the woman against the shower curtain, a naked arm dripping with water reached around the end of the curtain.

The wet hand closed about the gun.

Mason swiftly stepped back out of the range of vision.

65

"Hello," he called. "Anybody home?"

"Who . . . who's there?"

"Hello," Mason called. "This is Perry Mason."

"Oh . . . are you alone?"

"Yes."

"I was taking a shower. How did you get in?"

"I rang the doorbell. No one answered. I pushed against the door and it came open."

"Oh," she said, "sometimes that latch doesn't click. Just sit down, Mr. Mason, and make yourself at home for a few minutes, but you'd better close that door into the bedroom. I'm definitely not decent."

"I have to see you," Mason said, "right away."

She laughed. "Not *right* away."

"There isn't any time to waste," Mason told her.

"My, but you're terribly impatient. Close that outer door, will you please, Mr. Mason, and make sure it's locked this time. And now the bedroom door, please. I'll be with you in a second or two, just as soon as I dry myself and put on a housecoat."

He closed the bedroom door, made certain the outer door was locked, then went over to the desk. After going through the contents for some ten seconds, he could find no sign of the notebook he had seen earlier in the day.

He crossed back to the chair by the table and waited.

After some four or five minutes the door from the bedroom opened. Lucille Barton, wearing a housecoat of dark velvety material which outlined the curves of her figure, came gliding toward him.

Mason rose to meet her.

She hesitated a moment, then, smiling a full-lipped smile, gave him her hand.

Mason drew her to him and put his arm around her.

"Why, *Mister* Mason, I didn't expect this of *you*."

Mason's hands moved swiftly.

"Why, Mr. Mason, *what* are you looking for?"

"At the moment," Mason said, "I'm looking for a gun."

"Oh." Her voice showed a very definite change of expression.

"Where is it?" Mason asked.

She said, "You saw me, didn't you, Mr. Mason? You saw me through the shower curtain."

"I saw the gun on the bath stool," Mason said. "Where is it?"

"In my bedroom in my handbag."

"Let's go take a look at it."

"I'll get it."

"*We'll* get it."

"What's the matter, Mr. Mason? Don't you trust me?"

"No."

"Why, Mr. Mason, what's come over you?"

Mason said, "I'm getting cautious, that's all."

"Why, Mr. Mason," she said laughing, "that's what Arthur Colson says about me. He says I'm *too* cautious."

"And what," Mason asked, "brought up that subject of conversation when you were talking with him?"

Her light laughter was her only answer. She opened the door, led the way into the bedroom and said, "Honestly, Mr. Mason, this is *terribly* unconventional."

She moved over toward the bed, suddenly grabbed for the handbag.

Mason beat her to it.

She said sharply, "Mr. Mason, don't you take that gun away from me. Don't you try to . . ."

"What do you want a gun for?" Mason asked.

"For protection."

Mason took the gun out of the handbag, pulled the catch which enabled him to open the cylinder and slipped the cartridges into his pocket. Having done that, he snapped the cylinder back into place, returned the empty gun to her purse.

"Why, Mr. Mason, you mustn't do that."

Mason said, "Let's talk."

"But we *are* talking—you're not listening."

"Where did you get this gun?"

"It was given to me."

"By whom?"

"Mr. Hollister . . . No, I can't tell you. Please don't ask me."

"How long have you had it?"

"For two or three weeks."

"Why did Hollister think you needed it?"

"That's—that's something I can't tell you, Mr. Mason."

Mason said, "Let's start getting a few things straight, Lucille. I don't like to have anyone try to slip something over on me."

"No," she said, "I presume not."

"You told me that you were engaged to Mr. Hollister."

"Yes, I'm going to marry him."

"Where is he now?"

"You mean *right* now?"

"Yes."

"I don't know. Up in the northern part of the state somewhere."

"You don't know where? He doesn't call you?"

"No. You see I don't have a telephone, Mr. Mason. That's the bad part of this old-fashioned apartment house. There's no way he *can* call me. He'll drop me a letter. There's probably one in the mail now."

"You love him?"

"Mr. Mason, *why* are you prying into my private affairs this way?"

"Because I want to find out something about you and about some of the things that are going on."

She said, "Mr. Hollister is a gentleman. I care for him very deeply. I certainly respect him. He's a speculator who deals in oil properties. He'll take business trips for a week or two at a time, then he'll be back here in the city for perhaps—oh, sometimes as long as a month."

"And when he's gone, you start playing around with Arthur Colson?"

"Why, *Mister* Mason!"

"Well?" Mason asked.

She shook her head, and said, "No, it's not that way. Authur's just a business partner, but why are you so curious?"

"Because I want to find out. I have to know what's going on."

"Why?"

"Because I think it concerns me, and I think there may be more to this than you know about—or else you're trying to slip a fast one over on me."

"Why, *Mister* Mason! I don't know what you're talking about. You've acted in the *most* mysterious manner ever since you came in here this morning. I . . . I would like very much to have you negotiate this alimony matter with my ex-husband, Willard Barton, but I'm not going to permit you to make a lot of nasty insinuations just because I want you to do that for me. Of course, naturally, I respect you."

"All right," Mason said. "Under those circumstances tell me more about Arthur Colson."

"What about him?"

"I want to know all about him. Not the business part, the other."

"Heavens, he's just a friend. He's more a friend of Anita's than he is of mine."

"Who's Anita?"

"Anita Jordan, a girl that I know."

"Describe her."

"She's small, with very dark eyes, and nice dark hair. She likes to dress smartly and—you'd like her. She's just as cute as can be."

"All right. Now we've talked about everything else, let's come back to the question, and talk about Arthur Colson."

"What about him?"

"How long have you known him?"

"Not very long. He—he's an inventor. Sort of the dreamy, studious type. We have difficulty getting him to relax and do any—well, any playing around. He likes to read. He'll spend nights in research work at the library, reading. Then he'll go home and make plans and pound away on his typewritter."

"What does he invent?"

"Oh, lots of little gadgets. He's made money out of some of them."

"What sort of gadgets?"

"Well, right now he's working on something in connection with infrared rays. Before that, he worked out a device that opens and closes doors and does things like that."

"What do you mean?"

"It works with invisible light, what I think they call a black light. A beam runs across the room and as soon as some object crosses that beam it closes a circuit and does things—oh, for instance, like making electrical contacts so that the minute you walk into the house the electric stove clicks on and starts cooking, the radio turns on, and lights come on, and . . . I don't know, Mr. Mason, I think it's just a gadget. So many of his things are scientifically fine, but impractical when you want to work with them."

"And what's your interest in him?"

"It's just as I told you. I'm financing him."

"And why did you put up money for his inventions?"

"Because I think it's good business."

"And he's here until after midnight at times?"

"Well, sometimes when Mr. Hollister isn't here, and I . . . oh, Arthur gets blue and lonely. You see, he makes it a rule to take only one day a week for relaxation. I'm trying to get him to take his evenings off. He's definitely not the type that knows *how* to play. He's dreamy and abstract, and sometimes he can be something of a bore.''

"But he likes Anita Jordan?"

"Yes."

"And she likes him?"

"I guess so. Anita's—well, Anita's selfish in a way. You know, she wants security. I think she'd like very much to have someone marry her and settle down. I've tried to tell her that marriage doesn't mean security, but you can't argue with a girl about a thing like that."

"No," Mason said, "you can't. Now, suppose you quit lying, Lucille, and tell me who bought this gun for you."

"I think you're attaching a perfectly exaggerated importance to that gun, Mr. Mason."

Mason said, "When a woman takes a bath and has a gun on a stool right beside the bathtub, I feel that she's the one who's attaching an exaggerated importance to the weapon."

"Someone has sworn he's going to kill me. Arthur is afraid and I'm afraid."

"Who's that someone?"

"You wouldn't know him."

"You can't be certain," Mason said. "I know lots of people. What's his name?"

"His name is Pitkin—Hartwell L. Pitkin. He's a tough, coarse, uncouth individual. I made a mistake and married him when I was just a kid. I was only eighteen at the time, not old enough to have any sense about me. He had batted around and I felt he was a man of the world who could give me everything I wanted. I'd lived more or less of an isolated existence in a small town and . . .''

"How long did you live together?"

"Between two and three years."

"Then what?"

"Then I ran away."

"What do you mean, you ran away?"

"Just that."

"Did you get a divorce?"

"Eventually, but at the time I left him, I just ran away."

"With someone?" Mason asked.

"You're terribly direct, aren't you, Mr. Mason?"

"Were you with someone?" Mason repeated.

"Yes," she said, meeting his eyes.

"So what happened?" Mason asked.

"Hartwell swore that he'd follow us, find us and kill us both. He couldn't find me. He never did. I changed my name and then I got a divorce in Reno and . . ."

"And what happened to the man you ran away with?"

"He was killed in the war. I loved him."

"And then what?"

"He left me some insurance and—well, I married Willard Barton."

"All right, now tell me about Hartwell Pitkin."

"He . . . he's found out I'm in the city. Not the address yet."

"He's here in the city?"

"Yes."

"Where? What's he doing?"

"He's working for a man by the name of Stephen Argyle. He lives at 938 West Casino Boulevard. He doesn't know that I know where he is, but I found that out—and the worst of it is, Mr. Mason, that Ross Hollister and this man, Argyle, belong to the same club, play cards together and all that.

"Now you can see my predicament. Even if I should marry Ross Hollister it wouldn't really *solve* anything. You can imagine how a man like Ross would feel if he realized he'd married the ex-wife of his friend's chauffeur. It would humiliate Ross, and his friends would laugh at him . . . and Hartwell Pitkin is crazy jealous.

"Oh, Mr. Mason, it's a mess!"

"Now," Mason said, "I am beginning to understand."

"What do you mean by that?"

Mason gently but firmly pushed her toward the door of the bedroom. "Get some clothes on, Lucille. We're going places."

"Mr. Mason, why are you so . . . so grim?"

"Because you've been trying to slip something over."

"I have not!"

"Did you get all this furniture as spoils from your last marriage?"

"Don't be silly. It's a furnished apartment."

"Oh, I see. They furnish Oriental rugs, antique desks, and . . ."

"All right. If you *have* to know, I'll tell you about those. I saw you stretching your neck when you came in here this morning. Ross Hollister likes the good things of life. He intends to keep his place in Santa del Barra after we're married, but he wants to keep this place up too. He's an expert on furniture and interior decorating, and gradually he's bringing down bits of furniture he can spare from his place in Santa del Barra.

"That rug, for instance, came in Sunday. And his snooty old housekeeper had to wire me yesterday morning asking if he'd given me an Oriental rug. As though it's any of *her* business! She comes in by the day and goes home at four-thirty. Ross takes his dinners out, but he pays her just as much as if she were there all the time. I can tell you one thing, when we're married that woman is going to go— *fast!*"

"Why did she wire *you?* Why not ask *him?*"

"Because he left Santa del Barra at six o'clock Monday to lease secretly some lands on which he has a very confidential report from a geologist. He's a whiz at . . ."

"All right," Mason interrupted. "We'll hear more about him later. Right now go get some clothes on. You're going places."

Chapter 9

Mason held the door open for her and they walked down the steps together.

"I wish you'd tell me where we're——" She stopped abruptly.

"What's the matter?" Mason asked.

"That's my car!" she exclaimed.

"Where?"

"That sedan over there."

"You're certain?"

"Of course I'm not absolutely certain. It *looks* like my car."

"Just which one is it?"

"Right across the street, the one parked down next to the alley. The light brown sedan with the red wheels and the white sidewalls."

"All right," Mason said, "let's go take a look and see if it's yours."

They crossed the street. Lucille walked around to the left-hand side of the car, opened the door, and said, "Good heavens, yes! This is my car *and my keys are in it.*"

"Don't you usually leave your keys in it?"

"In the garage, yes. I leave the garage door locked and my keys are in it then, but whenever it's parked on the street I *always* take the keys out."

"Didn't you use the car today?"

"No."

"How did you get to my office?"

"In Arthur's car."

74

"All right, what do you want to do with your car—take the keys out and leave it here, or . . . ?"

"I want to drive it right back into the garage where it belongs."

She climbed in behind the steering wheel, angrily twisted the ignition keys, and jabbed her foot on the starter.

The starter whirred, the motor caught, raced for a moment, backfired, sputtered, raced and backfired again.

"Perhaps you have your choke too far out," Mason said.

"The choke isn't out," she said.

"I'll walk around to the garage," Mason told her, "and open the doors. That motor certainly doesn't sound right."

"Well, it doesn't *feel* right. I don't know whether someone's playing a joke on me or what, but—Arthur's a good mechanic. He was supposed to put new wiring on the car and—I don't know *what* he did. It was running all right, only the wiring was a little worn."

"It's probably connected wrong," Mason said. "You can drive across through the alley and up to your garage. I'll walk over and open the door. I guess you can get the car that far. Then we'll look under the hood and see what's wrong."

He walked across the street and up the alley.

Behind him, he could hear the car sputtering, banging and backfiring as Lucille Barton nursed it across the street. Then the shaft of her headlights illuminated the garage doors. Mason flung back the right-hand door, groped on the inside for the catch which held the other door, then suddenly paused in mid-motion.

The beam of headlights from Lucille Barton's car illuminated the legs of a sprawled figure which was stretched out on the floor of the garage. The shadow of the door hid the rest of the man's body.

Abruptly the motor slowed and almost instantly sputtered and died.

Lucille Barton, jerking open the left-hand car door, came out from behind the wheel with one swift, leg-revealing motion. She dashed over to Mason's side. "What's that?" she demanded. "Who's in there?"

Mason said, "That seems to be a man who's either sleeping, drunk or dead. Suppose we take a look."

He found the chain catch on the inside of the door, pulled it down far enough to release the door, swung it open a few inches, then stopped as reflected light from the headlights gleamed on the sinister pool which had welled out from the bullet hole in the man's head.

"Apparently," Mason said, "he's dead."

She took a tentative step forward, then suddenly drew back. Mason could hear the hissing intake of her breath.

"Well?" Mason asked.

"What kind of a frame-up is this?" she demanded. "What have you been doing? What kind of a deal are you trying to rig up on me?"

Mason, moving so that he could look down on the features of the dead man, said, "I think, Lucille, we'll put the question the other way. What sort of a deal have *you* been trying to frame on *me*?"

She said, "I'm beginning to see it all now—this whole business, this . . . all this stall about the gun and the car and the garage, and . . . so *that's* why you wanted to go in the garage."

Mason frowned, said nothing, but stood looking down on the body of Hartwell Pitkin who, by Lucille Barton's own admission, had been her first husband. He was now very evidently quite dead.

Lucille, looking past him, suddenly recognized the man. "Oh, my God!" she exclaimed, and flung her arms around Mason's shoulders to steady herself.

Chapter 10

Mason said, "Lucille, you're going to have to notify the police."

She stood looking at him with startled, suspicious eyes.

"Now, then," Mason went on, "when you tell your story to the police, try and make a better job than you did when you told it to me."

"What do you mean?"

Mason said, "Let's look at it from the police viewpoint. The man who is lying dead on the floor of that garage stood between you and everything you wanted in life. You had a chance to marry Ross Hollister. You couldn't do it as long as Pitkin was alive. It took his death to clear the way for you to proceed with that marriage. Why beat around the bush about it?"

"Are you trying to insinuate that I'm—that I'm responsible for—for this?"

"I'm not," Mason said, "the police will."

"Oh, Mr. Mason," she said, clutching his arm, "why did this have to happen to *me?*"

"It hasn't happened to you yet," Mason told her. "It's happened to Pitkin. Now leave the car here. Come on in and telephone the police. You'd better switch off the lights on your car. Aside from that, leave everything just the way we found it. Come on now, we'll go in and telephone the police."

He took her arm, gently pulled her away from the vicinity of the body, then escorted her down the alley and up the steps of the apartment house.

"You have your key?" he asked.

"Yes."

She fitted the key into the outer door, opened it and entered the lobby.

"There's the phone booth over there," Mason said. "You have a dime?"

"No, I don't think that . . ."

"Here's one. Call police headquarters. Tell them you want to report finding a body in your garage."

"You're going to stay with me?"

"No, I can't."

"I'll have to tell the police you were with me when we found him."

"That's right—when we found him. Now go telephone."

She walked a half a dozen steps toward the booth, then hesitated, turned, saw Mason's eyes were on her, and reluctantly walked the rest of the way to the booth.

Mason watched until she had dropped the coin and started dialing, then he hastily stepped back through the door, dashed down the short flight of steps to the street, and walked as rapidly as he could to where his own car was parked.

He drove to a drugstore, parked his car, called the unlisted telephone in his office.

"Hello," Della Street said.

"Argyle still there?" Mason asked.

"He went out to telephone and hasn't returned."

"How long ago?"

"About five minutes."

"When you got there you saw his Buick and the chauffeur waiting?"

"Yes."

"How long ago?"

"It was just after five o'clock, about an hour ago."

"How did you know it was Argyle's car?"

She laughed. "I noticed the license number. This case

78

has made me license-number-conscious. I find myself constantly peering at numbers."

"Argyle's been there up until five minutes ago?"

"Yes. He went down and dismissed the chauffeur right after I came in, then came right back."

"How long was he gone?"

"Not over a couple of minutes. Why?"

"I can't tell you over the phone, Della. When Argyle comes back get rid of him. Tell him I won't be back any more tonight."

"But I thought you wanted to see him."

"I did, but I don't. I can't tell you details. Wait there for me."

"Okay, anything else?"

"No. That's all. Be seeing you. 'By now."

Chapter 11

Della Street said, "Good heavens, what's the hurry, chief? What . . ."

"Where's Argyle? Did you get rid of him?"

"I didn't have to. He went out to telephone and didn't come back. What's all the excitement about, chief?"

Mason said, "The chauffeur's name is Hartwell Pitkin. It now turns out that he was Lucille Barton's first husband. They were married some seven or eight years ago. She ran off with a man and later divorced Pitkin. Now then, apparently as soon as Argyle dismissed Pitkin and while I was out at Argyle's house, Pitkin went to the address of Lucille Barton. His body is now in her garage. He was shot in the front of the forehead. Judging from the evidence, the shooting took place right where he fell in Lucille's garage."

"And you're going to . . . to represent this Lucille Barton?"

Mason grinned, "Not on your life, Della."

"That's fine," she said, relief in her voice.

"For once in my life, Della, when I talk with the police, I'm going to put the cards absolutely and squarely on the table. Lucille Barton isn't my client in any sense of the word. I advised her to tell the police the truth. *I'm* going to tell the police the truth."

"About the keys? About your search and . . . ?"

"About everything," Mason said. "Get those letters out that we received in answer to the ad in the paper. Here are the keys, Della. You can put the keys with the letters. We'll tell the police about the call this afternoon, about the license number in the notebook, about everything. You know, Della, I *could* be in a spot on this thing and I want to get out of it."

"How soon will the police be here?"

"That depends."

"On what?"

"On how many questions they ask Lucille Barton. Let's get this stuff out and then go have some dinner. After that, we'll come back here and wait for the cops. In the meantime, I want to start Paul Drake doing some work."

"What?"

"I'll show you," he said.

Mason picked up the telephone, dialed the number of Drake's office and when he had Drake on the line, said, "All right, Paul, here's a rush job for you. I want you to find out about a Smith and Wesson .38 revolver number S65088. Find out when it was sold, who bought it, and everything you can about it. I also want you to find out something about Argyle's chauffeur. A man by the name of Hartwell Pitkin."

"Why the gun?" Drake asked.

Mason grinned into the telephone and said, "Because sweetheart, it looks as if someone had tried to get Perry Mason all tangled up in something."

"And you don't want to get tangled?"

"I not only don't want to get tangled," Mason said, "but I don't intend to get tangled. I like to pick my cases rather than have them thrust upon me. Get the information and relay it to me just as soon as you can. Della and I are going out to dinner. When we return we'll probably have a date with the police."

"Want to tell me about it?" Drake asked.

"No. It's better for you to remain entirely innocent."

He hung up the telephone, said to Della Street, "Come on, Della, we're going out to eat. At least we won't be facing the police on an empty stomach."

"And for once," Della Street said, relief in her voice, "we can face them with a clear conscience."

"Oh, that's a cinch," Mason said. "Our conscience is *always* clear. Sometimes our motives are a little obscure and at times I have to hold out something."

"Yes. Quite a lot," Della Street observed. "Where do we eat?"

"Some place not too near here," Mason said. "Some place where the police won't find us in the middle of the meal and make us leave a half-finished filet mignon."

They walked down the corridor, passed Paul Drake's lighted office, took the elevator to the street and Mason hailed a taxi.

"We'll leave my car in the parking lot," he explained, "then the police will know we intend to be back. That will save them from wasting a lot of time and energy."

They went to a quiet restaurant more than a dozen blocks from the office, a place where there were curtained booths, an atmosphere of quiet seclusion, and good food.

More than an hour later, Mason finished his last cup of coffee, said to Della Street, "Well, how about it? Do you feel up to facing the police?"

"I feel up to facing anything."

"Okay, let's go."

They found a taxi, returned to the office building, and Mason said casually to the night operator of the elevator as they were whisked up to his floor, "Anybody looking for me, Sam?"

"No, sir, not a soul," Sam said.

Mason exchanged swift glances with Della Street, said, "I guess we'll take a look in Paul Drake's office, Della."

They found Paul Drake sitting in the little cubbyhole which was his private office, a desk littered with telephones in front of him.

"How are you coming, Paul?" Mason asked.

"Okay," Drake said, "I found out the dope on that gun

for you. It was sold to a jobber here in the city and by the jobber sold to a dealer out in the mountains about a hundred and thirty miles. The Rushing Creek Mercantile Company."

"To whom did the Mercantile Company sell it?" Mason asked.

"Don't know. It's a little place up there, and they fold up the sidewalks. I can't get any action on the phone."

Mason said, "Hang it, I need that information. Rushing Creek? That's a little resort and lumbering village, isn't it?"

"That's right. Quite a few trout fishermen go up there. It's also the gateway to some nice picnic and camping grounds back in the mountains."

"Well," Mason said, "keep after them. See if you can find out anything. You haven't heard anything more about Argyle—or that chauffeur of his?"

"Argyle's house is dark," Drake said. "I have a couple of men on the job. I'm working on the chauffeur's background."

Mason said, "Okay, stay with it, Paul. Let me know as soon as you find out anything."

He walked down to his office with Della Street, said, "Gosh, Della, the police must be *really* giving her a third-degree."

"Would she tell them about you?"

"I told her to."

"Do you think she did?"

"She had to. I was with her when she discovered the body."

Mason unlocked the door of his office, switched on the lights, sat down at his desk, started drumming with his fingertips . . . "I'll tell you what, Della. *You* wait here. Hold the fort. I'll take a quick run out to the hospital and tell Bob Finchley that we're coming along all right. You stay right here and if the police come, tell them you're waiting for me, that I'm out working on a personal injury case. And you can pave the way for a series of very pleasant relations with the police by showing them the ad we put in the *Blade*, telling them about the accident case, and showing them the letters we've received, and then giving them the keys."

"And tell them about Argyle?"

"Sure, the whole thing."

"Okay," she said, "I'll wait here and do my stuff with the police. Will it be the men from Homicide?"

"That's right, Homicide—probably Lieutenant Tragg."

"I like him."

"Don't make any mistake about him," Mason said. "He's smart."

"What difference does it make, if we're going to tell him everything we know?"

"I guess it won't make any," Mason said, grinning. "It's simply that I'm not accustomed to all of this law-abiding frankness. They'll be as puzzled as I am. They'll feel we're holding out something and have a nervous breakdown trying to find out what it is . . . Okay, Della, I'm on my way."

Chapter 12

Mason walked down the linoleum-covered hallway of the hospital.

Nurses had begun to quiet the patients down for the evening. The lights were dim and the hospital hush was broken only by the occasional rustle of starched uniforms as nurses on rubber-soled shoes moved swiftly and efficiently about their business.

Mason, feeling embarrassingly healthy, tiptoed awkwardly down the corridor.

The supervising nurse frowned at him, said, "No visitors after . . ." then, recognizing him, smiled and said, "I think your patient is feeling very *very* fine this evening, Mr. Mason."

"How come?" Mason asked.

"This afternoon he was worrying about the hospital bills, wondering how he was ever going to pay them, and . . ."

"I told him I'd take care of all those," Mason said.

"I know, but he didn't want you to do that, Mr. Mason. You've been terribly good to him, and of course he didn't have the faintest idea of who'd hit him. Those hit-and-run cases are really terrible things."

"And what happened to make him feel good this evening?" Mason asked.

She smiled. "The man who hit him came up and acknowledged the fault and was just ready to do anything on earth."

"Man by the name of Caffee?" Mason asked, frowning.

"I don't know what his name was."

"A man with thin features, gray hair, a gray double-breasted suit, about fifty-five or fifty-six . . ."

"That's the one," she said.

"Humph," Mason grunted. "I hope he didn't slip anything over on Bob Finchley. I'd warned that boy not to make any . . . oh well, let's go take a look."

The lawyer forgot to tiptoe. His heels were pounding belligerently on the corridor as he pushed open the door of Room 309. Bob Finchley, lying flat, with an elaborate system of pulleys holding his leg and hip in position, looked up, saw Mason, and a big grin engulfed his features.

"Hello, Counselor."

"Hello, Bob. How's it coming?"

"Fine, Mr. Mason. Gosh, we're all out of the woods! You know what happened?"

"What?"

"The man that hit me came in. He's really a swell guy. He had a young fellow with him from the insurance company, a chap about my age, who was really swell."

Mason said, "You should have called me."

"Gosh, I tried to, Mr. Mason, but your office was closed."

Mason frowned. "All right, Bob. What happened?"

"Well, this man told me that there was no need of my going to court. He wanted to know what I thought it was going to cost me for doctors and hospital bills and then the man from the insurance company said they felt pretty bad about it and—do you know what they did, Mr. Mason?"

Mason drew up a chair. "Look here, Bob. Did you sign anything?"

"Why, sure. I had to in order to get the settlement."

Mason's face darkened. "You mean you sold me out, Bob? You settled without me?"

"No, no, Mr. Mason, I fixed it so everything was all right for you. They really paid off."

"What happened?"

"The insurance adjuster said that he'd pay me five thousand dollars; that they'd pay all my hospital bills, all of my doctor's bills, and that they'd agree to pay you a reasonable sum as an attorney's fee."

"A *reasonable* sum," Mason said.

"That's what they agreed."

"Of course," Mason said, "my idea of what's reasonable and their idea of what's reasonable might be very far apart under the circumstances."

"And in addition to that," Bob said, "the man gave me his personal check for a thousand dollars over and above what the insurance company would pay."

"A man by the name of Caffee?" Mason asked.

Bob's face showed surprise. "No, not Caffee—Stephen Argyle."

"What!" Mason exclaimed.

"That's right."

Mason said, "Begin at the beginning. Tell me the whole thing. Make it quick, Bob. Get it out just as fast as you can. Did they give you a copy of the document you signed?"

"Yes, sir."

"Let me see it," Mason said.

Mason glanced through the document. A slow grin came over his features. "All right, Bob. Now tell me what happened."

"Well, they came in here about an hour and a half ago, Mr. Mason. It seems that Mr. Argyle was very, very much upset. He said he couldn't talk about the accident, because the insurance company wouldn't let him, but he was just terribly sorry about everything. He was a nice guy."

"Go ahead," Mason said.

"Mr. Argyle is really trying to do the right thing, Mr. Mason. He told me he'd been waiting at your office for you to come in because he wanted to have you with him when he talked with me. He said your office was closed but your confidential secretary was there and that she wasn't certain you'd be back any more this evening.

"He tried to call you from the hospital here two or three times but there was no answer."

Mason frowned. "We don't answer the phone after the office closes. I have an unlisted phone in my private office. I had no idea of what Argyle wanted. I was out on another case."

"Gee, Mr. Mason, I hope I didn't do anything wrong."

Mason shook his head and smiled. "On the contrary, Bob, you did just right."

"Gosh, I'm glad of that! The way you acted at first . . . well, I wasn't sure."

Mason pocketed the signed copy of the release, said, "Usually whenever anything like this happens, we tell the client not to make any independent settlement, because the lawyer can make a better settlement than the client can ever hope to. But this time, because we didn't know who had hit you, and it didn't look as though there'd ever be much chance of finding out, I neglected to give you the usual warning. How's your head? Hurting much?"

"No, its feeling swell. . . . Gosh, Mr. Mason, I hope I didn't . . . hope I didn't . . ."

"Not a bit," Mason said grinning. "That signed receipt you have releases Stephen Argyle for any and all claims you may have against him for his own acts and/or those of his agents from the beginning of the world to date."

"Well, isn't that receipt all right?"

"Sure, it's all right," Mason said, "but now remember, Bob, don't sign anything else. No matter who comes to you with anything, or what offer is made to you, don't sign anything. Understand?"

"Why, yes, sir."

"Now the insurance company gave you a check, and Argyle gave you a check?"

"Yes, sir. That's right."

"And what about your mother?"

"They're going to see her. They had me telephone her. They asked me if I thought a thousand dollars would cover the effect of her shock. . . . I knew Mom would be tickled to death with that settlement, but I looked thoughtful, and then Mr. Argyle said, 'And I'll raise that another five hundred dollars by my personal check.' So I guess they're making a settlement with Mom."

Mason said, "That's fine, Bob. Now I want you to endorse those checks and give them to me. I'm going to see that they're deposited to your credit first thing in the morning. You have an account?"

"Just a small one. Just a few dollars that I'd been saving up for my next year in college, in the Farmers and Mechanics National."

"All right," Mason said. "Write on the back of those checks 'Endorsed for deposit to my account,' then sign your name on them, give them to me, and I'll have my secretary take them down and deposit them to your account first thing in the morning."

"Gee, Mr. Mason, that'll be swell! Tell me, honestly, did I do wrong in making this settlement?"

"Under the circumstances," Mason said, "you did all right, but don't do it again. If anybody comes with anything for you to sign, no matter what it is, just tell them you're not signing a thing. Can you do that?"

"Yes, sir. I think so."

Mason took out his fountain pen. "All right now, endorse those checks. Be sure to endorse them only for deposit so that in that way nothing can be done with them except to put them to your account."

"Well, Mr. Mason, how about your fee? Are they going to . . ."

"You're damn right they are," Mason said, handing him the fountain pen. "They usually think they're pulling a fast one when they tell an injured party they'll pay a 'reasonable' attorney's fee. They offer the lawyer some absurdly small amount and then point out he'll have to sue to get any more. By the time they get done they whittle the thing down until . . ."

"Gosh, *Mr. Mason*," Finchley exclaimed in dismay, "they aren't going to do that to you, are they?"

"No," Mason said, smiling, "they aren't going to do that to me. You see, Bob, the insurance people were so afraid they'd admit liability that they made these releases read that they still denied their policyholder had actually inflicted the injury, but were making a settlement just to avoid litigation."

"Well, isn't that all right?" Finchley asked.

"Sure, it's all right," Mason grinned, "particularly because their policyholder really *didn't* inflict the injury. Tomorrow we'll make another settlement with the man who *really* hit you. And in the meantime we'll deposit these checks.

"And *that* should teach the insurance company not to sneak around behind a lawyer's back.

"Now you go to sleep, Bob."

And Mason gently closed the door to the patient's room.

Chapter 13

Whistling a tune, his hat pushed jauntily to the back of his head, Mason opened the door of his office and found Della Street pounding away at her typewriter.

"For heaven's sake," Mason exclaimed, "you do enough work during office hours. When I leave you here like this at night to keep an eye on things, don't try to ruin your nervous system by pounding away at that typewriter."

"This was some stuff that's important, and . . ."

"And your health is important too," Mason said. "This job isn't particularly easy on the nerves. What happened to the police, Della?"

"I don't know. I haven't heard a peep out of them."

Mason frowned. *"That's* something I can't understand. They should have been here hours ago."

"You didn't hear anything?"

"No, I've been out at the hospital."

"How's Bob Finchley?"

Mason grinned and perched himself on the edge of his desk. "Now there, Della," he said, "we have the bright spot of my entire legal career."

"Tell me about it."

Mason said, "The better class of insurance companies are always willing to deal with a lawyer, but there's a certain type of adjuster who loves to cut a lawyer's throat."

Della Street nodded.

"Obviously," Mason went on, "they figure they can settle with a client a lot cheaper than they can with a lawyer, and if they can get the client to make a settlement by assuring him that they'll agree to pay his lawyer 'a reasonable fee' the client thinks that's all there is to it. He doesn't realize that the insurance company will then offer the lawyer a nominal fee and tell him to file suit if he wants to get any more.

"That puts the lawyer in the position of having to throw in a lawsuit in order to get what's really coming to him and even then a jury is usually inclined to look at the thing from a layman's viewpoint, so he takes the offer and grits his teeth.

"A lawyer has a lot of overhead. He has to keep his office running and when he handles a personal injury case, he has to get a pretty good fee from the ones he wins in order to compensate for all of the time, energy and money spent in connection with the ones he loses."

"Are *you* trying to tell *me* the financial problems of running a law office?" Della demanded. "If you could see the bookkeeping headaches I have with five people on your payroll . . ."

Mason grinned. "No, Della, I'm simply feeling so darned good that I have to begin from scratch."

"Well, then," she told him, smiling, "by all means proceed from scratch." She pushed her chair back and came over to sit on the desk beside Mason. "All right, what happened?"

"The long arm of coincidence is playing right into our hands, Della."

"How come?"

"Evidently Argyle's chauffeur must have had the car out on the third and hit someone. He went to Argyle and without telling him any details let Argyle know he was in a mess. So Argyle decided to be smart, took the car out, parked it in front of a fireplug and then went to the club and reported it as being stolen. And to make his story stand up, bribed the doorman to say he hadn't been out all afternoon."

Della frowned. "Then Argyle's chauffeur was the one who was driving the car that hit . . ."

Mason grinned. "Don't be silly. It was Daniel Caffee, but Argyle *thought* his chauffeur was guilty."

"So what happened?"

Mason said gleefully, "I can see by the twinkle in your eyes that you know what happened, but you don't want to rob me of the pleasure of telling you about it. And believe me this is a *real* pleasure."

"Go ahead," she said, smiling, "tell me all the sordid details."

"Well," Mason said, "Argyle evidently got in touch with his insurance carrier and some young adjuster came out. This young adjuster was full of vim, vigor and vitality, and anxious to make a record with the main office. So he put the ideas in Argyle's head. They consulted records of traffic accidents, found out the name and address of the victim, learned what hospital he was in, and went out there."

"When did they do this?"

"Apparently," Mason said, "we can make a pretty good pattern. Almost immediately after I talked with Argyle he jumped in his car and came up to my office. He was waiting here for me when you arrived. Then he went down and dismissed his chauffeur. His chauffeur proceeded to go out and get himself murdered, and . . ."

"Yes," Della Street prompted, as Mason came to a frowning stop.

"Damn it," Mason said, "I'm so tickled about that insurance business that I'm letting my mind get away from the murder."

She placed her hand on his, gave a firm, steady pressure. "Go on, chief. The murder doesn't mean anything to *us*, but this insurance business does."

Mason pushed back his chair. "It's beginning to worry me. Why the deuce do you suppose the police haven't been in touch with me?"

"I can't guess."

"Well," Mason said, getting to his feet. "We're going to find out. We'll just drive casually down South Gondola Avenue and see how much excitement is going on, how many police cars are parked there, and so forth. If the police cars are still there, we'll know they're grilling Lucille Barton in her apartment. If the police cars have gone, we'll find a crowd of curious people still standing around in doorways, and we can get out and walk around and pick up enough bits of conversation to know what happened."

"Let's go," Della Street said.

Mason held her coat for her. She put on her hat in front of the mirror, and Mason, putting on hat and topcoat, switched off the office lights.

Mason stopped in Drake's office long enough to say, "Okay, Paul, we're leaving now. You haven't found out anything new?"

"Yes, I have, Perry."

"What?"

"I have a hunch your friend, the chauffeur, Hartwell L. Pitkin, is a blackmailer."

"The devil!"

"Nothing a hundred per cent definite at this time," Drake said, "but one of my men has uncovered an associate of Pitkin's, a friend who is a little more than a casual friend, and that chap intimated that Pitkin is making money from some source, that it's cash money, that it comes in large quantities and that Pitkin doesn't need to hold his job as chauffeur unless he wants to, that he's only holding that job as sort of a blind to divert suspicion from himself."

Mason gave a low whistle.

"So," Drake said, "my operative put the screws on this chap and found out as much as the fellow knew, which wasn't a great deal, but it indicates Pitkin may be shaking someone down."

Mason exchanged significant glances with Della Street. "A woman?" he asked.

"I wouldn't know," Drake said. "If it's a woman, she must be someone who has a reasonable amount of money, because Pitkin seems to be pretty well heeled with cash—that is, no really *big* money, but he can always pull out a roll with two or three hundred dollars in it."

Mason said, "Well, keep on working, Paul, but don't lose any sleep over it. If you've got your men out, let them do the work."

"I'm about ready to knock off," Drake said. "Getting a bunch of men out on an investigation is a job. What about Argyle? Do you want me to keep on him?"

"No," Mason said. "I've changed my mind about Argyle. You can take your men off the house and let Argyle do whatever he wants. I'll drop in and see him sometime within the next two or three days, and after he recovers from my visit, he'll know he's had a shock."

"You certainly seem to be sitting on a cloud," Drake said.

"I'm sitting on a cloud and the cloud's right on top of the world," Mason grinned. "You might find out something about Pitkin—anything you can—hell, Paul, there must be *something* . . . oh, well, never mind. Want to hear what happened?"

Drake said hurriedly, "Don't tell me. I don't want to know."

"Well," Mason said, "call your men off Argyle. He isn't important any more. I'd like to find out a little more about Pitkin, and in the morning you can find out about that gun. I wish you could have found out about it tonight."

"I think I can get something on that," Drake said. "I have a man who does work for me who lives in Santa del Barra. It's about eighty miles from there to Rushing Creek and I got hold of this chap and told him to go up to Rushing Creek and see if he couldn't get hold of the proprietor of the

Rushing Creek Mercantile Company. It's probably a one-man concern."

"Okay," Mason said. "Let me know if you hear anything. Come on, Della. I'll take you home. Don't lose any sleep, Paul. It's not that important."

"Okay," Drake said. "I'll keep in touch with the office by telephone and let you know if I get anything."

"Don't call me if it's later than an hour from now," Mason said. "I'm going to roll in. Good night, Paul."

"Good night."

Mason escorted Della out of the office, down to his waiting automobile, said, "Well, let's just drive by the neighborhood and see what's doing, Della."

"You want me to drive?"

"No, I'll drive."

Mason slid in behind the wheel of the automobile, nodded to the parking station attendant, gunned the car, and rolled out of the parking station to the street. He piloted the car with deft skill through the late traffic and swung into South Gondola Avenue.

Mason said, "Okay, Della, keep your eyes open. I'll drive slowly. You see how many police cars you can spot."

"Which place is the apartment house?"

"The one at 719. It's in the middle of the next block on the left-hand side, and . . ."

"Oh, yes, I have it spotted now."

"Quite a few cars around there," Mason said.

He drove slowly across the intersection.

Della said, "They seem to be private cars. I don't notice any police cars. Would they have red spotlights on them?"

"That's right, and long radio antennas. Gosh, Della, I don't see a one."

"Well, they've probably taken Lucille down to Headquarters for questioning and . . ."

"But the neighborhood would hardly have quieted down this soon," Mason said. "I'm going to drive very slowly.

As I pass the entrance to the alley we'll take a good look at the garage and see what's around there."

Mason slowed the car almost to a stop.

They looked up the alley. The row of garages was dark and silent, illuminated only by such light as filtered in from the street lamps.

"Hey, wait a minute," Mason said, "something's wrong."

"What?" Della Street asked.

Mason braked his car to an abrupt stop. "Sit over behind the steering wheel, Della," he said. "Here, give me the flashlight out of that glove compartment. No, wait a minute. I'm going to drive in there. I think we can drive in and then back and turn around."

"Chief, what's wrong? What do you think . . ."

"I don't know," Mason said. "There's something fishy about the whole business."

"If there is, hadn't you better keep out and . . ."

"I have to find out what it is," Mason said.

He looked back to make certain the road was clear, backed a few feet, then turned the car so it was headed toward the garages, and slowly entered the alleyway.

He drove to the garage bearing the figures 208, said, "Okay, Della, you sit here. Give me that flashlight."

Mason took the flashlight, jumped out of the car, approached the garage, saw that the doors were closed but unlocked. Mason eased the right-hand door back a few inches, and flashed the beam of the light into the interior of the garage.

Abruptly, he ran back to the car, jumped in, threw the flashlight over on the back seat, backed the car swiftly, and turned it around.

"What's the matter?" Della Street asked.

"Everything," Mason said grimly. "We're hooked!"

Chapter 14

Della Street said nothing until Mason had gained the street once more, turned the car sharply to the right, and urged the motor into speed.

"What is it?" Della Street asked.

"That little devil!" Mason said. "That double-crossing little devil!"

"You mean she didn't report to the police?"

"She didn't report to the police," Mason said. "The body is lying in there on the floor just as I saw it, only *now* there's a nice shiny gun right beside his right hand."

"So it will look like suicide?"

"So it will look like suicide."

"Well?" Della Street asked.

Mason said, "I've got to find a place where I can park this car and do a little thinking, Della."

"Can't we just forget about the whole thing?"

"That's what I'm trying to figure. Let's . . . here's a parking place. Let's stop here for a minute."

Mason eased the car into the parking place and switched off the motor and the headlights.

They sat for a while in silence.

"After all," Della Street said, after two or three minutes, "no one *knows* that you were there except Lucille Barton, and *she* certainly can't talk."

Mason said thoughtfully, "Someone is masterminding this thing. Someone has talked her into playing smart."

"Well, *you* told her what to do."

"I told her what to do," Mason said, "but remember I

also have a responsibility. I saw the body. And when I saw the body there was no gun near it."

They were silent for another few minutes, then Mason said suddenly. "Start asking me questions, Della."

"What about?"

"About this darned case. Let's try and clarify it."

"Well," Della Street said, "suppose you *don't* tell the police? Then what will happen?"

"Then," Mason said, "the police will find the body— that is, *someone* will find the body and report it to the police."

"Who?"

"Probably Lucille Barton."

"I don't get you."

"She'll come driving home with some witness, probably her girl friend, Anita Jordan."

"Why not the boyfriend?"

"Because she's engaged, and if she's going to get her name in the papers she wants it to appear she spent the evening with a girl friend."

"I see. Go on. Then what?"

"Then," Mason said, "Lucille Barton will ask Anita to open the garage. Anita will open the doors, the headlights from the automobile will illuminate the interior, Anita will scream, Lucille will scream, they'll have mutual hysterics, notify the police, and put on an act for the benefit of spectators and officers."

"Can they get away with it?"

"I don't know," Mason said. "It depends on how good a job they've done."

"You mean Anita and Lucille?"

"No, Lucille and whatever person was acting as mastermind—probably Arthur Colson."

"You want me to ask questions about him?"

"About anything. Just throw questions at me."

"Won't the police ask her if she knows this dead man?"

Mason thought that over. "Yes. And she'll have to admit that she does. She'll have to admit that he was her ex-husband. Then police will want to know why he picked her garage as a place in which to commit suicide. They'll immediately become suspicious about whether the death is or is not a suicide, and . . . Then, of course, later on they'll fire a test bullet through the gun and compare it with the fatal bullet—if they can find the fatal bullet. Then they'll know the gun in the garage was a planted gun. That won't look good."

"All right," Della Street said. "Now, I'll take the opposite approach. Suppose you *do* tell the police."

"Then," Mason said, "I'm in a jam."

"Why?"

"Because I told Lucille to report it, but I didn't stick around long enough to make sure that she followed my instructions."

"Are you responsible for her?"

"No," Mason said, "but I'm an attorney. I'm an officer of the court. I know I'm supposed to report any bodies I find. I found one and simply told Lucille to report it."

"And what will Lucille say?"

"That's the hell of it," Mason said. "Lucille will have to insist that we didn't find any body, and that I'm now trying to protect some client by making her the fall guy."

"Will the police believe her?"

"If they do I'm in a jam. If they don't they'll raise hell with me because I didn't make certain the body was reported, and because I didn't check later when police didn't contact me."

"Well, why didn't you?"

"Because," Mason said, "of that damned insurance business. I was so tickled with what had happened and the way Argyle had slipped one over on himself that I didn't pay enough attention to the fact police hadn't called on us. Hang it, Della, if I'd had my wits about me I'd have known what must have happened. Well, the logical thing to do, the only thing I can do as a law-abiding citizen and as an officer of the court, is to report to the police."

"Well, why don't you do it then?"

"Because," Mason said, "the police are laying for me. They wouldn't want anything better than an opportunity to trip me up, and I have a feeling I'm fighting someone who is in a position to trip me up if I do make such a report."

"I'm running out of questions, chief," Della Street said.

"I've already run out of answers, Della."

They sat for a while in silence, then Mason started the car.

"Well?" Della asked.

"I'm hooked," Mason said. "I have the answer now."

"What is it?"

"Whoever is directing this thing is smart. There's only one way I can save myself."

"What's that?"

"We've got a client."

"Who?"

"Lucille Barton."

"I don't get it."

Mason said, "As her attorney anything she said to me would be privileged. They can't ask her about it and they can't ask me about it."

"What about what you *saw?*"

"If she tells the police about it she'll be acting on my advice. If she doesn't, there's no way of proving I was there."

"I don't like it," Della Street said.

"Like it!" Mason exclaimed, "I *hate* it, but I'm hooked with a client, Della. Show on the books I'm representing her on a question of alimony with her last husband, one Willard Barton.

"And now, I'm going to drive you home."

Chapter 15

Paul Drake was waiting in Mason's office the next morning when Mason came in.

Della Street flashed Mason a warning glance and took his overcoat and hat.

Paul Drake studiously avoided Mason's eyes, said, "I've been trying to call you, Perry. Della thought you might be in early this morning so I decided to wait. It's about this man, Hartwell L. Pitkin, you wanted me to look up."

"Oh, yes," Mason said. "I saw the papers this morning. Seems he committed suicide in the garage of Lucille Barton's apartment house."

"That's what the papers said, Perry."

"Strange coincidence, isn't it, Paul?"

"Certainly is. She'd been married to him years ago."

"To Argyle's chauffeur, Paul? Good heavens, you mean that . . ."

"That's right," Drake interposed, still refusing to meet Mason's eyes.

"What other details do you have, Paul?"

Drake said, "Sometimes, Perry, you get so damn smart that you have us all running around in circles and meeting ourselves coming back."

"I don't get it," Mason said.

"There are lots of goofy things about the case. The police received a report from Lucille Barton. She was hysterical. She'd opened the garage door to put her car away for the night and found the body. She had a girl friend who was going to spend the night with her. They didn't touch anything but left the car right there with the motor running and beat it to the telephone in the apartment house. They notified the police."

"I see," Mason said.

"Hartwell L. Pitkin had been shot with a .38 caliber revolver," Drake went on, methodically. "The gun was found by his right hand."

"So I saw in the paper, Paul. No question that it's suicide?"

"The police are investigating."

"What do they think?"

"They aren't taking me into their confidence."

"No, I suppose not."

"Now then," Drake said, "I have some other information for you."

"What?"

"That gun you wanted to know about, the Smith and Wesson .38 number S65088."

"Oh yes, what about it, Paul?"

"Well, that gun was sold, just as I told you, to a jobber who in turn sold it to the Rushing Creek Mercantile Company.

"A chap by the name of Roscoe R. Hansom is the proprietor of the Rushing Creek Mercantile Company. The revolver was sold about a month ago to a man who signed the gun register as Ross P. Hollister."

Mason said, "That's interesting."

"You don't know the half of it," Drake went on.

"No?" Mason asked, settling himself back in his swivel chair. "What's the other half, Paul?"

Drake said, "I got that information last night. You remember you were in a hurry, and I had a man from Santa del Barra drive up to Rushing Creek. He managed to get Hansom out of bed and talked him into going down to the store and looking at the records. Of course you were in a hurry to get the information, and—well, that's the way it is. When you want things in a hurry, you want them."

"Right you are," Mason said, grinning. "No use dilly-dallying around. So you got the information. Thanks a lot, Paul. That's good work."

"And," Drake went on, "naturally the fact that we were in such a hurry for the information impressed Mr. Hansom."

"Well, naturally," Mason said. "However, I fail to see what connection *that* has with the matter. If he wants to live out in the country and go to bed with the cows and chickens he'll have to realize that *we* can't gear *ourselves* to *his* schedule."

"Oh, sure, sure," Drake said, "but I just thought you should know."

"Why, Paul?"

"Because," Drake said, "when the body of Hartwell L. Pitkin was found, the gun with which he had either shot himself, or had been shot, was lying by his right hand. Someone who had a nice little emery wheel had ground every number off the gun, the number on the tang, the number on the inside of the cylinder mechanism, the numbers that are on the little concealed places, everywhere."

"Well, well," Mason said, his voice showing relief. "Then they couldn't trace the gun, Paul?"

Drake kept his eyes averted. "But the guy who had filed off the numbers didn't know too much about guns. On that model of gun, the Smith and Wesson, the number of the gun is also stamped on the inside of the wooden grip. You have to take a screw driver and remove one of the wooden grips to see it."

"Go on," Mason said.

"The police did that. They found the number. It was S65088.

"Of course, the police got busy and started tracing the

number. When they got Roscoe Hansom out of bed for the second time to find out about the sale of the gun, naturally Hansom wanted to know if it had become a habit, and . . ."

"The devil!" Mason said, straightening himself abruptly in his swivel chair, and frowning.

"Exactly," Drake said. "Of course, Hansom didn't know the name of my operative from Santa del Barra, but he has a pretty good description and putting two and two together, the police are apt to make four at any moment. When they do, you're going to have some explaining to do.

"Now, then," Drake went on, still avoiding Mason's eyes, "there are two or three other things you should know about."

"Okay, Paul," Mason said, his voice sharp with anxiety, "let's hear them. Spill 'em fast. I may have to start moving."

Drake said, "Naturally, the police wondered why no one had heard the sound of the shot. Quite evidently the shot had been fired there in the garage. The nature and extent of the hemorrhage shows the man dropped almost immediately when the shot entered his brain."

"Go ahead, Paul."

"They made inquiry around and found that one of the automobiles was doing a lot of skipping, backfiring, and banging. It caused some annoyance on the part of the occupant of the building across the alley. He looked out of the window. It was beginning to get dark, but he saw a man and woman standing in front of the garage at 208. The man was a tall, distinguished-looking gentleman with a light topcoat. The woman was wearing a plaid coat, had a dark hat. They were opening the door of the garage. They had some conversation and then the motor was shut off and they walked away and left the car there. The car had been making a terrific noise from a series of backfires, and police think the shot must have been fired at about that time. If that's true, of course, that would make it murder. A man would hardly have committed suicide in the presence of two witnesses; and if he had, and the witnesses didn't report it—well, you can see the police reasoning."

"Go ahead," Mason said.

"Now then," Drake went on, "when the police answered Lucille Barton's call, they found she was wearing a plaid coat and a black hat. On the strength of those garments, the witness now makes an idenfication of Lucille Barton as being the woman he saw. Lucille denies that she was anywhere near the garage at that time."

"What time?"

"Somewhere around six o'clock. The witness isn't positive as to the time."

"What about the man?" Mason asked.

Drake said, "So far, they have only a general description of the man, but when police fingerprinted the gun they found a print on the inside of the gun where someone had probably been holding it while he tried to remove the numbers, or it *could* have been in ejecting shells. They think it's the print of a man's right index finger. It's a pretty good print."

"I see," Mason said.

Drake said, "By pulling a lot of wires with the newspaper boys I was able to get a photographic copy of that print."

He reached in his pocket, pulled out a wallet, took out a small photograph of a fingerprint, handed it to Mason, and said, "That's enlarged about three times, Perry."

"Any other fingerprints?"

"No. The outside of the gun had been wiped clean of fingerprints, but apparently the person who had been handling it forgot to remove the fingerprint on the inside."

"I see. Anything else?"

"Some other stuff," Drake said, "but I don't know what it is. The police are suspicious about the whole setup. They're particularly suspicious about Lucille Barton. She

106

was out with a girl friend named Anita Jordon. Anita knows Lucille, and she knew Hartwell Pitkin. She gives Lucille an alibi, but for some reason she isn't too happy about it. Police have an idea she's going to weaken on her alibi before they get done with her."

"A lot of commotion," Mason said, "over the mere finding of a body under circumstances which would indicate suicide."

"The trouble is," Drake said, "that when they went through the pockets they found around five thousand dollars in nice crisp currency. There was a package of hundred-dollar bills which still had the sticker from the bank wrapped around them, and the initials of the cashier. The police traced that money and found it had been drawn out a few days ago by a Mr. Dudley Gates. Dudley Gates is a business associate of the Stephen Argyle who employed Pitkin as his chauffeur. He's also a friend of this Ross P. Hollister, who seems to have bought the gun and then gone out on a business trip and neglected to communicate with any of his friends telling them where he'd be. Dudley Gates apparently accompanied Hollister."

Mason pinched out his cigarette, drummed nervously on the edge of the desk.

"That's probably all right, Paul. I happen to know something about Ross Hollister. He's a sharpshooter who handles oil leases and investments of that sort. He's on a business trip and he'll communicate with his friends by mail. His girl friend doesn't have a telephone so he usually drops her a line as soon as he gets located, or sends her a telegram and lets her know where his is."

Drake said, "Well, I got a little stuff on Hollister. He lives at Santa del Barra, divorced, decree not final for a couple of months yet. Has a nice place there, a housekeeper comes in by the day. She comes early to get breakfast, goes home at four-thirty. Hollister was there Monday when she left at four-thirty, but was expecting to leave at six that night. She hasn't seen him since. His business trips usually take about ten days. She never hears from him while he's gone. That oil lease business is secretive."

"And Dudley Gates is with Hollister?"

"That's right. Argyle, Gates and Hollister are partners of a sort. Hollister is the big shot. The other two guys are yes men."

"It's all tied in with that damn apartment of Lucille Barton's," Mason said.

Drake said, "Well, that's the general situation. Of course, finding all that money on a corpse is bound to attract attention, and naturally police are going to wonder about the cash transaction between Dudley Gates and Hartwell Pitkin."

"And police are interviewing Stephen Argyle?"

"Yes, they got Argyle up out of bed early this morning and started talking with him. Argyle says the last time he saw his chauffeur was out here in front of your office. He says he had driven to your office to see you and left his car outside. Then when he realized you weren't in the office, and weren't apt to come in within the next few minutes, he went down and told the chauffeur to take the car and drive it back to the house, put it in the garage, and then Pitkin could have the night off."

"Well?" Mason asked.

"Apparently Pitkin did just that. He must have driven the car out to the house and put it in the garage. It was there this morning when Argyle went out to look for it after the police had got him out of bed. By the police time schedule that would have put Pitkin back in Lucille's garage at just about the time the witness heard the car doing all the backfiring. The man must have been talked into entering the garage— and he was killed as soon as he walked in."

Drake got up out of the chair. "Keep that photograph of the fingerprint if you want, Perry. I'll let you know about new developments."

...on said, "However, in the event any action should be ...against Mr. Caffee, he would doubtless want to apply ...Court of Probation, and the Court would be very ...influenced by the sort of settlement which had been ..."

...le said, "Well, of course . . ."

...ffee said, eagerly, "Why do you say 'in the event' ...should be any criminal action?"

...Mason stretched and yawned. "Well, of course, someone ...ld have to sign a complaint in order to start a criminal ...secution. I don't *know* that anyone's going to sign a ...mplaint. On the other hand, I don't know that anyone is ...ing to fail to sign one, so I said, 'in the event.'"

...Caffee looked at Ingle. Ingle looked at Caffee.

...Ingle said, "Well, of course, as far as the insurance ...ompany is concerned, we can't consider these extraneous ...atters. We have . . ."

"You can consider the circumstances in a case, can't ...you?"

"What do you mean?"

"The bearing they'd have on a jury?"

Caffee coughed nervously. "I wonder if I could speak with Mr. Ingle privately, Mr. Mason. I think . . ."

"Sure," Mason said. "Della show the gentlemen into the law library. Take you time, gentlemen."

Della Street arose and, crossing the room, opened the door into the law library.

Ingle and Caffee filed out of the office.

Mason closed his right eye in a wink at Della Street.

She closed the door, came back and said, "What's going to happen when they find out there have been *two* settlements, chief?"

"Damned if I know," Mason said. "After all, we don't have much in the line of a precedent in such matters. It's usually hard enough to get one settlement, let alone two.

"Thanks, Paul."

Drake said, "So long, Della."

"So long, Paul."

The detective left the office. Mason glanced at Della Street, said, "Hand me that ink pad from the rubber stamp outfit, will you, Della?"

She wordlessly placed it on the desk. Mason pressed his right index finger on the pad, then on a blank sheet of paper.

Della Street came to look over his shoulder and compare his fingerprint with the photograph of the fingerprint police had found on the gun which had been responsible for the death of Hartwell Pitkin.

"Good Lord, chief," Della Street gasped, her fingers digging into his arm.

"Take it easy, Della," Mason said. He pushed back his chair, walked over to the washstand, carefully soaped his hands, and removed all traces of the ink. "And I thought the guy who was masterminding this business was crude!"

Della Street picked up the inked impression of Mason's fingerprint, struck a match, burned the paper, and then crumpled the ashes in the ash tray.

"Where does all this leave *you*, chief?" she asked.

"Right behind the eight ball," Mason told her thoughtfully. "But that doesn't mean I have to *stay* there."

Chapter 16

Mason had just finished drying his hands when Gertie, the receptionist, announced that Daniel Caffee and the representative of his insurance company, Frank P. Ingle, were waiting to see Mason.

Mason hesitated, then said to Della Street, "Have Gertie show them in, Della."

Frank P. Ingle, a grizzled, gray-eyed shrewd individual, shook hands with Mason, turned to Caffee and said, "If you don't mind, Mr. Caffee, I'll do the talking."

"Not at all," Caffee said.

"I take it you're willing to talk this over, Mr. Mason," Ingle said, seating himself and smiling cordially.

"Certainly. Go ahead and talk."

"Perhaps you'd better *start* the talk, Mr. Mason."

Mason said, "Money talks, gentlemen."

"I know, I know," Ingle said hastily, "but the question is, Mr. Mason, how are we going to work out any standard for . . ."

Mason interrupted, "This boy's been seriously injured. I want three thousand dollars for doctors and medical expenses; I want five thousand dollars' compensation; I want two thousand dollars' attorney's fees; that's ten thousand dollars in the boy's case. I want two thousand dollars for the mother, fifteen hundred for a new car, and one thousand dollars' attorney's fees; that's a total of fourteen thousand five hundred dollars. I have Caffee's check for ten thousand. The insurance carrier can give me its check for the balance."

Ingle smiled. "Well, of course, M[...] understand that you *want* these things, [...] have a duty to our stockholders. It is, of [...] that the accident happened, but we m[...] practical businessmen. How about the ea[...] this boy? If *you* had been the one who had [...] of this accident, while the pain and suffering [...] been any more intense, nevertheless our [...] have been greater because *you* have a g[...] capacity.

"As a practical man, as a practicing attorney [...] you will recognize that the monetary limit of [...] bility is the loss of earning capacity, plus some [...] amount which will compensate for pain and suff[...] I would say that with a young, vigorous boy of [...] fifteen hundred dollars would be a *very* adequate c[...] tion for pain and suffering. Statistics show tha[...] ninety days at the outside he'll be back at work [...] earning capacity unimpaired. Even if we were to c[...] he could make three hundred dollars a month, let [...] from that amount he would have to pay room and [...] which are furnished him in the hospital, and . . ."

Mason interrupted, "I've heard all that line before[...]

"Doubtless you have," Ingle said.

Mason said, "I don't want to hear it again."

"Surely, Mr. Mason, you're not going to be arbitrary.[...]

Mason met Caffee's eyes, "I'm going to be arbitrary."

Caffee coughed, said, "After all, Mr. Ingle, there are circumstances in this case which . . ."

"Now let's not misunderstand each other," Ingle said hastily. "Whatever the responsibility may be for having failed to stop and render assistance, we are now discussing only the property damage."

"That's right," Mason said. "We're not compounding a felony or conspiring to conceal a crime."

There was a moment's uncomfortable silence.

"Right now, Della, the important thing is to get this settlement cleaned up while we're free to work on it."

"You mean while we're *free?*"

"That's right," Mason said. "Ingle thinks I'm pretty crude, but if he could only look under my hair and see what's going on in my mind, he'd probably faint."

"I'll say he would!"

Mason said, "We're practicing law with a stop watch in one hand and a time bomb in the other—a hand grenade with the pin pulled."

Mason started pacing the floor.

Della Street's eyes, sympathetic, loyal and understanding, followed him.

The door from the law library opened. The two men returned to the room. This time Caffee was in the lead, and Caffee did the talking.

"We'll make the settlement, Mr. Mason," he said. "The insurance company doesn't care to establish a precedent in such matters. It's angry with me for having given you that check and statement last night. I'll give you my check for the balance, and I'll make an adjustment with the insurance company later."

"Just so we get the money," Mason said.

Caffee whipped out a checkbook.

Mason said, "Let me look at those releases, please, Mr. Ingle."

While Caffee was making out checks, Mason looked over the releases. "These seem to be all right," he said.

Mason signed the releases, accepted the checks.

Caffee said, "I hope we understand each other, Mr. Mason."

"I think we do."

"You . . . well, Mr. Ingle says it will be better if I don't have any *definite* understanding."

"Exactly," Mason said, and shook hands.

Caffee said, "I can't begin to tell you how sorry I am this happened. It's been a lesson to me."

"I know," Mason said. "You probably didn't sleep any last night."

"Frankly, I didn't, Mr. Mason."

"We live and learn," Mason told him, arising and ushering them to the door. "I have sleepless nights myself."

Ingle said over his shoulder, "You're a fast worker, Mr. Mason."

Mason said, "Well, there's no use dillydallying around."

"No," Ingle said, as he was being all but pushed out into the corridor, "you don't dally, but you certainly are a dilly, Mr. Mason. *Good* morning!"

"Good morning," Mason said, closing the door.

Chapter 17

"Do you want me to run down and deposit those checks?" Della Street asked.

"No," Mason said. "I'm going to do that job myself. It'll give me a legitimate excuse to be out of the office for a while."

"And after that?" she asked.

"And after that," he said, "I'm going to have to think up another one. If I can't think of a legitimate excuse, I'll think of an illegitimate one and have to make it sound legitimate."

"Bad as that?"

"It may be."

The unlisted telephone rang. Della Street picked up the receiver, listened, said, "It's Paul Drake, chief. He wants to talk with you."

Mason walked over, picked up the receiver, and said, "Okay, Paul, let's have it."

Drake said, "You remember I was telling you about this man Hansom who's the proprietor of the Rushing Creek . . ."

"I remember," Mason interrupted.

"Well, the police decided they'd talk with him. Apparently they had a hunch somewhere, so they brought him down here and went over his gun register with him, and they don't like the looks of what they find."

"What do they find, Paul?"

"Well, in the first place, while the signature purports to be that of Ross P. Hollister, and the address and everything matches, the name on the gun register apparently was written by someone else. The specimens don't agree with Hollister's handwriting."

"What else?"

"And among other things, the police found that Lucille Barton was playing around a bit with a man by the name of Arthur Colson. Exactly what his relationship is isn't clear, but in any event, when Hansom was confronted with Arthur Colson, he made an immediate and positive identification. He says that's the man who bought the gun."

Drake quit talking, and Mason was silent for a while.

"You there?" Drake asked abruptly.

"I'm here," Mason said. "I'm doing a little thinking. Anything else, Paul?"

"That's all at present."

"What does Arthur Colson say?" Mason asked after a moment.

"Arthur Colson says it's a case of mistaken identification. He's squawking his head off. He said that if the police wanted to make any sort of an identification they should have put him in a line-up, and let this man Hansom identify him. Of course, the police realize that he has a point there. The police were simply exploring around when they stumbled on to this. However, they don't like what they're finding, and they're going to keep digging."

"Any chance it is a false identification, Paul?"

"Not a chance in the world. As I get the story, this fellow Hansom is a pretty shrewd old duck. He knows most of the customers who come in the store, that is, the regular customers. Along during the fishing season, there's quite an influx of people buying fishing licenses and all that, but this was off season. He remembers the transaction and he's absolutely positive of his identification. He certainly impressed the police.

"Why would Colson have signed Hollister's name?" Drake went on. "Have you any idea?"

"He had to sign *some* name," Mason said, "and since she's going to marry Hollister, or thinks she is, she'd hardly want to have a gun register showing the name of some other chap . . . From Colson's standpoint Hollister was the best and safest alias he could use."

"When you look at it that way, it all fits," Drake admitted.

"Anything else, Paul?"

"They made a paraffin test on Pitkin's hands. That, of course, isn't as conclusive as it might be, but nevertheless it means a lot where they get an absolutely negative reaction within such a short time after a gun has been fired."

"There was no reaction?"

"Not at all. Police did a good job on that one. They made the test before the body was moved. Something about the case made them a little suspicious."

"Do you know what it was, Paul?"

"I think I do, Perry."

"What?"

"You're not going to like this."

"Hell, I don't like any of it," Mason said.

"Well, there was quite a little spot of blood on the garage floor directly *underneath* the gun. Now of course it *could* have happened that way, but police are inclined to think it didn't. The man *could* have shot himself, then remained on his feet for a second or two, and blood *could* have spilled, and then he *could* have fallen over and dropped the gun. But you know how Lieutenant Tragg is, he's a thorough worker and a smooth worker."

"Yes," Mason said, "I know how he is. You aren't holding anything else back on the theory that you want to give me this stuff in small doses, are you, Paul?"

"That's all of it to date."

"Well, it sounds like enough," Mason said, and hung up the phone.

"What is it?" Della Street asked.

117

Mason said, "Whoever pulled off that job last night wasn't half as clever as I'd thought. But it's too late to worry now, Della. If Carlotta Boone, who gave us the tip on Caffee's license number, comes in, give her a check for one hundred dollars. Be sure it's a check and not cash. Tell her we need the canceled check for our accounting."

"So we can see where she cashes it and perhaps trace her if we have to?"

"That's right. Hold the fort, Della. I'm on my way."

Chapter 18

It was eleven o'clock when Mason returned to the office building.

One of Drake's men who had been lounging unostentatiously by the cigar counter casually moved forward so that he entered the same elevator with Perry Mason.

"Good morning, Mr. Mason," he said. "How's everything this morning?"

Mason glanced sharply at him, said, "Okay. You're one of Drake's men, aren't you?"

"That's right. Just going up to report."

Mason felt the man's hand brush against his and a card was deftly inserted between the lawyer's thumb and forefinger.

Mason pocketed the card, then said, "Hang it, there was a telephone number I was supposed to call. What the deuce did I do with it?"

He made a show of searching his pockets, then finally drew out the card which Drake's operative had just given him. He said, "Here it is," and held it in his hand so that he could read the message which had been written on it.

The card was in Della Street's handwriting and said, C.B. CAME IN. GOT CHECK $100. LOTS OF VISITORS—OFFICIAL—WAITING.

"Oh, well," Mason said, "I guess it's not too late. I'll call as soon as I get to my office."

The elevator stopped at his floor. Drake's detective entered the office of the Drake Detective Agency without a word, and Mason walked down the corridor and fitted his key to the lock of the door to his private office.

"Well, Della," he said, "I guess we've . . . hello," he exclaimed abruptly, as he saw the office was filled with people.

Lieutenant Tragg removed a cigar from his mouth, said, "Hello, Mason."

"Well, well, hello, Lieutenant! How are you? You seem to have quite a gathering here."

"Yes," Tragg said, "I think you know Lucille Barton and Arthur Colson. This is one of my plainclothes men here. Come in and sit down, Mason. We want to talk with you."

"Fine," Mason said. "How have you been, Tragg?"

"Sit down," Tragg said. "Make yourself comfortable. This may be a long session. I'm going to warn you, Mason, that you're not going to like this."

Mason smiled at Lucille Barton, who looked as though she hadn't slept all night. "How are you, Lucille? I see by the morning papers that you've had quite a shock."

"Yes," she said, her eyes avoiding Mason.

"How are *you* today?" Mason said to Arthur Colson.

"Fine," Arthur Colson said, keeping his eyes concentrated on the carpet.

"Where were you about six o'clock last night, Mason?" Tragg asked.

Mason smiled, shook his head, and said, "I can't remember offhand, Tragg."

"Well, start thinking."

"All right."

"Keep thinking."

"How long do you want me to keep thinking?" Mason asked.

"Until you think of the answer."

Mason frowned, settled himself behind his office desk, noticed Della Street's apprehensive eyes.

"Well?" Tragg said, after some two minutes.

"Haven't thought of it yet," Mason grinned.

Tragg's face showed concern. "Look, Mason, I like you. I want to give you the breaks, but I'm going to tell you something. This is murder, and you're in a different position than you usually occupy in a murder case."

"Indeed," Mason said. "Well, I'll have a cigarette. I notice you're smoking, Tragg. How about you people, want a cigarette?"

Two heads shook in silent unison.

"How about you?" Mason asked the plainclothes officer.

"No thanks."

Mason lit up, settled back once more in his chair.

"All right," Tragg said, "if you're going to take time to think, we'll make a record of how long you think." He took his watch out from his pocket, said, "Now then, Mason, I'm going to ask you for the second time. Where were you about six o'clock last night?"

Mason watched Tragg's eyes glued to the face of the watch, said, "I can't tell you, Tragg."

"Keep thinking," Tragg said.

"I *know* now where I was," Mason said, "but I can't tell you."

"Why not?"

"It would be violating a professional confidence."

"Having to do with what clients?"

Mason smilingly shook his head, "After all, Lieutenant, there are some things we can't discuss, you know. A lawyer has a certain obligation to his client."

Tragg, with a gesture of exasperation, put the watch away, said, "You were interested last night in a gun. A Smith and Wesson having the number S65088."

"Was I?" Mason asked.

"You know you were. You had a detective from Santa del Barra get in touch with Roscoe Hansom who runs the

121

Rushing Creek Mercantile Company and inquire about the sale of that gun."

"Well," Mason said, "if you want to make positive statements like that, Lieutenant, I certainly don't want to contradict you."

Tragg said, "I became interested in that same gun a short time later. I roused the telephone operator at Rushing Creek out of bed and got her to get Roscoe Hansom out of his bed. Your man had just left about half an hour before with the information."

"Indeed."

"Why were you interested in that gun?"

"I wanted to find out who had purchased it."

"Why?"

"For various reasons."

Tragg said, "That gun was involved in a murder. The murder was committed around six o'clock. The body wasn't found until around ten-thirty. Now then, Mason, *how did you know the gun was going to figure in a murder case as early as nine o'clock?"*

"I didn't," Mason said, his voice and manner showing complete surprise.

"Your man must have left Santa del Barra even before nine o'clock."

"Probably considerably before," Mason said. "If I had been interested in the gun, and right at the present time I'm not prepared to admit that I was, Lieutenant, it would have been because of its importance as evidence in a civil matter. And I, of course, had no inkling that it had been used in a murder."

"Oh, certainly *not*," Tragg said, sarcastically, "but just what *was* your interest in the gun?"

"I'm sorry, Lieutenant, I can't tell you that."

Tragg's face showed concern. "This is a lot more serious than you think it is, Mason. I've got a whole fist full of cards that aren't on the table yet. It'll be a lot better if you come clean."

"Well, I'll answer any question I can," Mason said.

"When did you first become acquainted with Lucille Barton?"

"Yesterday," Mason said instantly.

"Did she get in touch with you, or did you get in touch with her?"

Mason said, "I'm glad you're asking me something I *can* answer. Della, where's that issue of the *Blade?* The one I had the ad in?"

Della Street arose, silently went to the files, opened one of the drawers, took out a folder, and handed Mason a copy of the ad in the *Blade.*

"Take it over to Lieutenant Tragg," Mason said.

Tragg regarded the ad, frowned and said, "What's *that* got to do with it?"

"Get that letter out of the safe, Della," Mason said. "The one that came to the Drake Detective Agency, the one that had a key in it."

"A key!" Tragg said.

"A key!" Lucille Barton exclaimed.

"A key," Mason repeated, smilingly. "A key—one you open doors with, you know."

Della Street brought the letter from the safe.

"Give it to the Lieutenant, Della."

Lieutenant Tragg took the letter, read it and frowned.

"We may just as well give it to Miss Barton," Mason said. "She wrote it, you know, Lieutenant."

"The hell she did," Tragg said, chewing on his cigar.

Della Street handed the letter to Lucille Barton, who read it, then passed it across to Arthur Colson.

"And what did you do about that letter?" Tragg said. "You waited until the hour mentioned when she was out of her apartment and then went to . . ."

"Don't be silly, Lieutenant," Mason interrupted. "You

don't think *I'd* use a key to open the door of a person's apartment without permission, do you? I immediately went to Miss Barton's apartment. I knocked on the door, rang the doorbell, and found that I'd caught her at rather an inopportune moment. However, she invited me to come in and make myself at home while she retired to the bedroom and finished dressing. Then she came out and we had a delightful talk and *that*," Mason said, glancing meaningly at Lucille Barton, "was where the relationship of *attorney and client* began. She requested me to represent her in a certain matter."

"Oh," Lucille Barton said.

"So you're representing Mrs. Barton?"

"Oh, yes," Mason said. "I believe she prefers to go under the name 'Miss Barton,' Lieutenant."

"So you're representing her," Tragg said.

"Why, yes."

"And what are you doing for her?"

Mason smiled and shook his head.

Tragg said, "Your activities yesterday, Mason, were rather peculiar."

"Why, I didn't think so, Lieutenant."

"You had a busy day, didn't you?"

"Fairly so. I usually keep pretty busy."

"You went out to 938 West Casino Boulevard. You met Stephen Argyle, and accused him of driving a car in a hit-and-run accident, didn't you?"

"I believe I suggested to him that his car might have been involved in an accident, yes."

"And while you were there you met Hartwell L. Pitkin?"

"Are you referring to Mr. Argyle's chauffeur?"

"Yes."

"He was there," Mason said.

"Now then," Tragg said, "when did you first see that gun—that Smith and Wesson number S65088, and why did you become interested in tracing it?"

"I'm sorry, Lieutenant. We were getting along fine, but *now* you're asking something I can't tell you about."

"Why not?"

"A privileged communication."

"Now then," Tragg went on, "the numbers on this gun had been ground off with a nice little emery wheel. One number had been overlooked, but it took a screw driver to get at it. The grinding of the metal looks like a very fresh job."

"Indeed?" Mason said courteously.

"Now when you became interested in this gun, how did you know the number?"

Mason smiled and shook his head.

"Was it before the numbers had been ground off, or afterwards?"

"I'm sorry," Mason said, smiling affably.

"It *must* have been before they were ground off, Mason, because that screw hadn't been loosened since the gun left the factory. I'm wondering if perhaps *you* weren't the one who removed the numbers."

Mason merely smiled, then stifled a yawn behind his hand.

Tragg nodded to the officer, said, "All right, bring that witness."

The officer pushed through the door toward Mason's reception room.

Tragg said, "I'm going to put it right on the line with you, Mason. I think that at six o'clock you were out in front of Mrs. Barton's garage at 719 South Gondola. I think a shooting took place there in that garage and I think you're trying to cover up that shooting. I think I have a witness who can identify you."

Mason tapped ashes from the end of his cigarette. "I feel quite certain you haven't any such witness, Lieutenant."

"This witness positively identifies Lucille Barton here."

Before Mason could say anything, the door was jerked

open. The plainclothes officer stood to one side and a tall man with a high forehead, high cheekbones, thin lips, and a long neck, entered the office in an apologetic manner as though ashamed of the intrusion.

Tragg pointed to Perry Mason, and said, "Is that the man?"

"I . . . . I don't know until he stands up," the man said. "You see, I never saw his face real clear."

Mason smiled at him and said, "I'm Perry Mason. What's your name?"

"Goshen—G-O-S-H-E-N," the man said, "Carl Evert Goshen. I live next door to the place where the murder was committed and . . ."

"Never mind," Tragg said, "I just want to know whether that's the man."

"I can't tell until he stands and walks around. I can tell you then."

"Stand up," Tragg said to Mason.

Mason grinned. "That's a hell of a way to make an identification, Lieutenant. You'd better have some sort of line-up if you want to have an identification that's worth anything."

"I can't get you in a line-up without arresting you," Tragg said. "I don't particularly care about doing that until I'm certain of my ground. If this witness identifies you, then I'm certain of my ground."

"That's not only getting the cart before the horse," Mason said, "but it's putting him in circular shafts and letting him chase the tailboard."

"Shut up," Tragg said. "I'm doing this."

"Indeed you are," Mason said.

"Get up," Tragg insisted. "If you're innocent you have nothing to fear."

Mason tilted back in his swivel chair, smiling at Tragg

"How was he dressed?" Tragg asked Ghoshen.

126

"Just like I told you, he had on a light topcoat, tan-colored, and a gray hat."

Tragg said to the officer, "There's the coat closet there. Get out his coat and hat."

Mason said, "Now, wait a minute, Tragg. You know you haven't any right to do that. You can't . . ."

"The hell I can't," Tragg said, and then, turning to Goshen said, "When this witness gets up to try and stop the officer, you notice particularly the way he walks, the way he moves . . ."

Mason said, "I'm telling you, Lieutenant, this is an invasion of my rights as a citizen."

The officer opened the door of the coat closet, suddenly stopped, hesitated for a moment, then turned back to face Tragg.

"Go on," Tragg said impatiently, "get out the coat and hat. We'll put it on him, if we have to. He's going to stand up and . . ."

"I'm sorry, Lieutenant, but . . ."

"Get that coat out!" Tragg said.

The officer brought out the topcoat. It was a heavy black coat Mason had never seen before.

"Get out the tan one," Tragg said.

"That's the only one in here, Lieutenant."

Mason flashed a glance at Della Street. She was cherubic in her innocence.

"That's not the coat," Goshen said, positively.

Tragg said suspiciously to Mason, "Where did you get that coat?"

"I didn't get it. You did."

"Well, then, where did you get that lead to Stephen Argyle? How did you know it was *his* car that was mixed up in the accident?"

Mason merely smiled and shook his head. "Lieutenant, you keep asking questions which are predicated on false premises. I'm sorry, but Argyle's car really *wasn't* mixed up in the accident."

"I thought you . . ."

"I really thought it was," Mason said, smiling, "but you know how it is, Lieutenant. Lots of times you'll think you have all the evidence in a case and start making charges, accusations and wild assertions, and then suddenly find out, much to your chagrin, that the facts were entirely different, and . . ."

"Never mind all that," Tragg said. "I want to know where you got the information, why you went out and told Argyle his car had been in the accident, how you knew it."

Mason said, "As a matter of fact, Lieutenant, the man who was involved in the accident is a gentleman by the name of Caffee—Mr. Daniel Caffee, 1017 Beachnut Street, Apartment 22-B. I located him yesterday evening and I'm quite satisfied that it was purely a mistake on Mr. Caffee's part. When Mr. Caffee learned that my client had been injured he was only too glad to make adjustments."

"What do you mean—adjustments?"

"He paid off."

"When?"

"This morning, after making a partial payment yesterday."

"I'll be damned," Tragg blurted.

"Of course," Mason told him, "I don't care to have that information noised about, Lieutenant. I'm merely trying to help you clean up a case in which you seem to be interested. I understand that Mr. Pitkin committed suicide in Miss Barton's garage."

"He was murdered in Miss Barton's garage."

Mason made clicking noises with his tongue against the roof of his mouth.

Tragg said, "You weren't in your office last night between five and six. Della Street showed up in a taxicab. Stephen Argyle was waiting here for you. His chauffeur was waiting down in front. Shortly after five o'clock, Argyle went down and told the chauffeur there was no need for him to wait. Argyle came back and waited here until almost six o'clock. Then he telephoned his insurance carrier and made an appointment to meet an adjuster in front of the building. He can account for every minute of his time, and he also knows that *you* weren't here in your office."

"I'm seldom in the office after five o'clock," Mason said. "I try to close up and get out. Of course, occasionally I do night work but I don't like to see clients after five o'clock. It establishes a bad precedent and . . ."

"And," Tragg went on, "the reason you weren't here is because you were with Lucille Barton. When Pitkin entered that garage, you were there. At any rate, you were there shortly after he entered. Now I'm willing to be fair about the thing, Mason. I think the evidence indicates that probably Pitkin was there for no good purpose. He may have attacked you or Miss Barton. One of you had a gun and pulled the trigger. That stopped the career of Mr. Hartwell L. Pitkin, and I'm perfectly willing to concede that it wasn't the career of an exemplary citizen. It was the career of a blackmailer, an opportunist, and a crook. If he was waiting there in that garage, I'm satisfied he was waiting for no good purpose, but I'm only going to give you this one chance to come clean privately. After this it will have to be publicly. I'm going to tell you frankly that, if it was self-defense, I'm willing to make allowances for that, but I want to clean this case up fast."

"Yes, I can understand that," Mason said. "And I know you want to be fair."

"Now, then," Tragg went on, "Lucille Barton says she was with you."

"She does?"

"That's right. At first she said she was with Anita Jordan, and Anita Jordan was to give her an alibi for the entire evening, but when we started getting right down to brass tacks that alibi blew up."

Lucille Barton said hurriedly, "I didn't say I was with Mr. Mason at six o'clock. At first I said I was with him just before I met Anita and . . ."

"Now *I'm* doing the talking," Tragg said.

"He doesn't want you to talk," Mason said meaningly to Lucille Barton. "Therefore, *as your attorney,* I would advise you to keep quiet."

"None of that," Tragg said to Mason. "I'm talking to you."

"And I'm talking to my client, Lieutenant."

"When were you with Mrs. Barton yesterday?"

"I told you I saw her sometime in the morning."

"When did you see her after that?"

"I'm sure I can't tell you the time, Lieutenant."

"But you *did* see her after that?"

"Oh, yes."

Tragg said, "All right, we'll quit beating around the bush, Mason. I want to take your fingerprints."

"Certainly," Mason said, "go right ahead. I'll be only too glad to co-operate in every way I can, Lieutenant; but of course you understand I can't betray the confidences of a client."

Tragg nodded to the officer, who produced a small fingerprint outfit from his pocket and approached the desk.

"Stand up," Tragg said.

"Oh, I'll do it sitting down," Mason told him smiling, extending his hand to the officer.

Goshen suddenly said, "I don't think that's the man. The man that I saw was not quite so heavy and . . ."

"Just step outside for a minute," Tragg said, "I want you to see this man with his overcoat on and I want you to see him standing up and walking. You can't make any identification while he's sitting down there behind the desk."

Mason said, "And I warn you, Lieutenant, he can't make

an identification that's worth a damn unless he picks me out of a line-up."

Goshen arose, paused uncertainly, then walked out through the door to the reception room.

Tragg said. "You can be tough about it if you want to, Mason, but there's an easy way of doing this and there's a hard way. If I can't do it the easy way, I'll do it the hard way."

"That's very logical," Mason said. "Now, where is it you want my prints, officer—on this piece of paper? Oh, yes, now I believe I'm supposed to roll each finger across the white paper."

Lucille Barton was regarding Mason with fixed intensity. Arthur Colson glanced at Mason, then hastily averted his eyes.

Silently, the officer took Mason's fingerprints.

"You can get up and wash the ink off your hands now," Tragg said.

Mason grinned. "No, thanks. Your witness might come popping in. Della, I think you have some cleaning tissues in your desk. You might bring them to me and I'll wipe the ink off my hands with those. No need to get the washbowl all smeared with ink."

Tragg said, "Try sitting there if you want to, but you can't stay there forever. You're going to have to leave this office sometime. I'll have the witness watch you walk through the foyer. I'll have him watch you at various places and if this fingerprint evidence comes out the way I think it's going to I may have him watch you in a shadow box."

Della Street handed Mason a box of cleaning tissue, and some cleansing cream. "Put the cream on your fingers, chief," she said. "Rub it in. That will clean off the ink."

"Thanks," Mason said.

The officer handed Tragg the fingerprints. Tragg took a photograph from his pocket, compared the fingerprints one at a time, then suddenly gave an exclamation of satisfaction. He whipped a magnifying glass from his pocket and began examining the prints more closely, comparing one of them with the print on the photograph.

Suddenly he said, "Mason, that's your fingerprint on that murder weapon!"

"Is it indeed?" Mason said.

"What have you to say to that?"

"Nothing."

"Mason, I'm going to tell you officially that gun was used to murder Hartwell L. Pitkin. I can now establish definitely that gun has your fingerprint on it. Now, then, in the face of that evidence, what have you to say?"

"Nothing," Mason told him. "I'm protecting the confidence of a client."

"You can't protect the confidence of a client to the extent of failing to explain your fingerprint on a murder weapon."

"There seems to be a difference of opinion about that," Mason said. "By the way, Della, Lieutenant Tragg didn't ask about that second letter. Miss Barton didn't tell him anything about that because she didn't know anything about it. *She* wrote the first letter to me, but that second letter must have been written by someone else without her knowledge."

"What letter are you referring to?" Tragg asked.

"Get that second letter, Della. The one that enclosed the key to the desk in her apartment."

Della Street once more went to the files, brought out the second letter, and handed it to Lieutenant Tragg.

"This letter came by special messenger," Mason explained.

Tragg read the letter, asked ominously, "There was a key in it?"

"Oh, yes," Mason said, "a key to the desk."

"Where is it?"

Mason said, "I have both keys right here, Lieutenant. Would you like them?"

132

Tragg took the keys which Mason handed across the desk, regarded them in frowning concentration.

"So you see," Mason said, "I quite naturally felt that Miss Barton wanted me to get the evidence, but didn't want to take the responsibility of being the one who gave it to me. So when she and Arthur Colson over there came to my office yesterday afternoon I took advantage of her presence here to slip down to her apartment and open the desk. Sure enough, the key fitted the desk and in the upper right-hand pigeonhole was a notebook and a gun. Now, Lieutenant, if you can find the person who wrote that *second* letter, you can go a long ways toward discovering the murderer of this man Pitkin, in the event your premise is correct and the man was murdered."

Tragg said, "By gosh, if you entered that apartment and started messing around in it, I can . . ."

Mason interrupted sharply, "Come, come, Lieutenant. Once more you're getting your cart and your horse all mixed up. I didn't enter the *apartment* without permission. Lucille Barton wrote that first letter and sent me the key. That certainly gave me permission to enter her apartment by using the key, which she had so conveniently placed at my disposal. But that second letter, that must have been a trap, Lieutenant. That . . ."

"You opened that desk," Tragg said. "Was that gun in there?"

"I will go so far as to say this, Lieutenant—*a* gun was in there. Now you can see what that means. The desk was kept locked. Someone had a key to that desk, a duplicate key. Someone sent me that key. Now, quite obviously, Lieutenant, since Miss Barton was here at the office at that time, and the gun was there in the desk at that time, Miss Barton *couldn't have been carrying that gun*. And if you didn't find her fingerprints on the gun you can't prove that she *ever* had it. But I really can't tell you anything more, Lieutenant. I've given you some hints. In fact, I think I've stretched a point in giving you some hints."

Lieutenant Tragg said suddenly to the officer, "Take Colson and this Barton woman out of here. He isn't talking to me. He's using me as a sounding board to tell these two what he wants them to say."

The officer rose abruptly. "Come on," he said to the others.

Mason said, "My advice to you, Miss Barton, under the circumstances, is to *say absolutely nothing*. In view of the hostile attitude of the police I suggest you refuse to answer any questions on the advice of counsel."

"On the advice of counsel!" Tragg said. "Wait a minute. Are you going to represent her in this murder case?"

"Is she accused of murder?"

"She may be."

"Well, as I pointed out to you," Mason said, "when I went to call on her at her apartment yesterday, she retained me to act as her attorney."

"For what?"

"That I can't tell you."

Tragg turned to Lucille Barton and said, "You didn't tell me that."

"You didn't ask me specifically," she answered evasively.

"Well, what was it you wanted him to do?"

"Tut, tut, Lucille," Mason said, wagging a warning finger. "Not a word, remember now, not a word."

She turned to Tragg. He face showed relief. "You heard what my lawyer just told me," she said.

Tragg said to the officer, "Get them out of here," and then chewed angrily on his cigar while the officer herded the pair out into the reception office.

Tragg scraped a match into flame on the sole of his shoe, lit his cigar once more, turned to Mason, said, "Mason, I don't want to drag you into this unless I have to."

134

"Thanks."

"But the way you're doing things, I'm afraid I'm going to have to."

"Yes, I can see that."

"You know what it will look like in the newspaper— LAWYER'S FINGERPRINT FOUND ON MURDER WEAPON."

"You feel you should release that information to the newspapers?"

"I'll have to."

"Yes," Mason said, "that certainly will make headlines."

"Then there'll be another headline LAWYER REFUSES TO EXPLAIN."

"Yes, I can see where that will make sensational newspaper reading."

"Hang it, Mason," Tragg said, "you and I are on opposite sides of the fence, but I don't want to crucify you. I'm not certain that you were the one who was with her when Goshen looked across there at the garage. If you were with her, I think it was because she'd got hold of you and dragged you out there to show you something and you didn't have any idea what it was. If you can explain that, for heaven's sake go ahead and explain it."

Mason said, "Let's follow that thought a little farther, Lieutenant. Suppose that's what did happen. Would that relieve me of responsibility?"

Tragg said, "I'm not prepared to give you a definite and final answer on that."

"Well, give me an indefinite and temporary answer."

Tragg said, "The time of death is particularly important. We can fix the time of death within an hour or so the way things are now, but *if* we'd been notified, say at six o'clock, we could have fixed the time of death almost to the minute. You had a duty to notify the police."

"Yes, I understand."

"Therefore," Tragg went on, "you'd have to take your

medicine on that. Now, *was* the body in the garage when you were called there at six o'clock?"

Mason said, "I've told you, Lieutenant, I can't tell you where I was at six o'clock."

"And if this man Caffee was the fellow who hit Finchley's car, how does it happen you strong-armed a settlement out of Stephen Argyle?"

"I didn't."

"He made a settlement last night with Finchley."

"That's right."

"That is something I checked up on rather carefully," Lieutenant Tragg said, "because naturally I was interested in accounting for his time during the afternoon and evening."

"And you were able to do it?"

"Sure. He was out at his house. You came out there and accused him of a hit-and-run. Naturally, he doesn't want to discuss the hit-and-run charge."

"I dare say he doesn't."

"But shortly after you'd left him," Tragg went on, "Argyle did some thinking and decided he'd better buy his way out. He rushed to your office. He had the chauffeur wait downstairs. Then, when it looked as though you weren't going to be in for a while, and Argyle remembered it was Pitkin's night out, he went back down to let the chauffeur go. He told him to take the car back to the house."

"I see."

"Argyle waited until around six o'clock, then telephoned the insurance people and told them where he was, and what he was doing. The insurance adjuster had kittens, told him to stay away from you and under no circumstances to talk with you. The adjuster said he was on his way up to the office just as quick as he could get there, so Argyle waited in the lobby. The man at the cigar counter remembers him distinctly. Argyle waited about five or ten minutes in the

136

lobby, and then the insurance adjuster came up and took him in tow."

Tragg studied Mason, added, "Of course, if Argyle's car didn't hit this guy, Argyle and the insurance company will naturally want a return of the money they paid."

"I'm quite certain they will," Mason said.

Tragg looked at him sharply. "You aren't saying specifically you're going to give it back?"

"That's right. I didn't say that. I'm not."

"What!"

"I'm going to hang on to it."

"Look," Tragg said, "why don't you take your hair down and come clean, Mason?"

"I don't like to take my hair down. It might get in my eyes."

"Well *something's* in your eyes now. Look, Mason, this woman didn't think you were her attorney when she came in here."

"The deuce she didn't!" Mason exclaimed apparently in surprise.

Tragg said, "If you come clean I'll do everything I can to see that you get a square deal, not only with the press but at Headquarters."

"And the district attorney?" Mason asked.

"And with the district attorney," Tragg said, but his voice suddenly lacked conviction.

Mason grinned. "You know as well as I do, Tragg, that if you could get anything on me, the district attorney would welcome you with open arms. The case against Lucille Barton would pale into insignificance."

"Well," Tragg said, "what do you think he's got against you now? He's got enough to throw the book at you."

"Let him throw," Mason said. "Just so he throws it across the plate. And you can tell him for me I'll knock it over the fence for a home run."

"Not with that fingerprint on that gun you're not going

to," Tragg said. "That gun was the one that killed Pitkin. I have a report from our expert in ballistics."

"Indeed?"

Tragg got to his feet. "Well, I gave you your chance, Mason."

"You sure did," Mason said. "Pardon me if I don't get up, Tragg. That man Goshen might come running in the door and put the finger on me. I don't like to be identified in that way. I always prefer to have some sort of a line-up. At least the witness should have *some* choice."

Tragg said, "Don't be a fool, Mason. You can't spend the next two weeks sitting down. We'll identify you sometime and when we do it's going to look like hell—the asinine way you tried to dodge."

Tragg stalked through the door of Mason's office out to the entrance room.

Mason exchanged glances with Della Street. "Good Lord, Della, that gun *was* the murder weapon!"

She nodded mutely.

"I'd felt certain that when they examined the fatal bullet they'd find it had been fired from another gun and . . . Della, where the devil did you get that topcoat?"

"It's Paul Drake's," she said in a low voice. "Gertie heard them talking while they were waiting in the reception room. I slipped down to Drake's office, borrowed his overcoat and left yours there with him."

Mason grinned. "Did Drake know what you wanted it for?"

"He didn't ask any questions—he was careful not to."

Mason said, "Della, raise your salary a hundred dollars a month, and come over here by my desk. *I* can't get up at the moment because Tragg may come busting in here again with that popeyed witness."

Chapter 19

Mason spread out the newspaper on his desk, said, "Well, they certainly did a job, didn't they, Della?"

Della Street nodded.

"Nice headlines," Mason said, reading them: LAWYER'S FINGERPRINT FOUND ON MURDER WEAPON—ATTORNEY REFUSES TO STAND SO WITNESS CAN MAKE IDENTIFICATION . . . BEAUTIFUL DIVORCEE ARRESTED IN MYSTERIOUS MURDER . . . LAWYER PROSSESSED KEY TO SUSPECT'S APARTMENT.

Mason looked up. "That sure is quite a smear, Della."

"'Smear' is no word for it. Incidentally, I've been wondering, why did you tell Lieutenant Tragg about those letters and give him the keys?"

"It was the only way I could tip off Lucille Barton to what I wanted her to say."

"I don't get it."

Mason said, "Suppose someone else had written *both* of those letters."

"Well?"

"Sooner or later," Mason said, "it was bound to come out that a key to the apartment had been sent to Paul Drake and that Paul Drake had turned that key over to me. Now then, if anyone else had sent that key and I used it to enter the apartment I was a lawbreaker. But if Lucille Barton herself had sent that key then I was entering the apartment with her permission."

Della Street nodded. "I see now. I wonder if she did."

"Once in the apartment with her permission," Mason

went on, "the situation was entirely different. So if I can get the idea across to her that *someone else* sent the key to the desk, and that the gun was kept in the desk, I've given Tragg something to worry about."

"Suppose she had sense enough to get it?"

"Darned if I know," Mason said, "but I wasn't trying to give her an out. I was giving Tragg something to worry about, also Colson. I wonder if Colson . . ."

Mason was interrupted by Drake's code knock on the door.

"Let Paul in, Della."

Della Street opened the door.

Paul Drake, carrying an afternoon paper under his arm, said, "Did you see what they had to say in . . . Oh, I see you have one."

"Sit down, Paul," Mason said. "Quite a smear, isn't it?"

"I'll say it's a smear."

Mason said, "This witness, Goshen, will identify me if he has half a chance. I don't want him to have that chance."

"You can't prevent it," Drake said. "Why didn't you let him do it in the first place? It's going to look like hell when he does it now."

Mason grinned. "You talk like Tragg, Paul. What does Hollister look like? You must have his description."

"He's around forty-seven or forty-eight, tall, rawboned, brunet, busy eyebrows. I've picked up a fair description and am trying to get a photograph."

Mason seemed surprised. "Well, well, there's another tall man who enters the picture. Perhaps Goshen saw him. And this Dudley Gates, who got some money out of a bank and turned it over to Pitkin. What does *he* look like?"

"He's a younger man, about thirty-three, medium height, stocky, blond, blue-eyed . . ."

"Well," Mason said, "we can probably cross him out of the picture, but Goshen certainly should see this man Hollister."

Drake's face lightened. "You *may* have something there, Perry. *Was* it Hollister?"

Mason said nothing.

The hope which had been on the detective's face faded. He said, "I'll withdraw the question."

"Okay," Mason told him. "How about Dudley Gates? Have they found him? What does he say about the money?"

Drake said, "Dudley Gates is with Hollister. They're partners, and they left Monday night to look over some oil properties."

"Where are these properties?"

"Up north somewhere. Naturally the location would be something they'd keep secret."

Mason said musingly, "This is Thursday, the sixth. They left on Monday. They've had three days. . . . What time Monday night, Paul?"

"Probably right at six o'clock. Hollister's housekeeper left at four-thirty. Hollister was waiting to see a man, then Gates was joining him, and he was leaving at six o'clock.

"The housekeeper heard him talking to Gates on the phone, and saying he was leaving on the dot at six, and Hollister was a stickler for punctuality.

"It would have taken Gates a little over an hour to get up there from here."

Mason said, "Paul, I've got to get out of this building without anyone seeing me."

"You can't do it," Drake said. "Tragg has this witness, Goshen, planted in a car with a police escort, waiting for you to walk out. Newspaper reporters and photographers are sprinkled all around the place."

"Paul, *you* keep *your* offices open twenty-four hours a day?"

Drake nodded.

"You have the only office in the building that is open all night?"

"Well?" Drake asked.

"I'm coming down and live with you, Paul."

"I don't get it."

"We're going to close up this office. Della is going to scout the corridors and make certain that there's no one between here and your office. Then I'm going down to your office. Della will lock up this place and start home. Naturally newspapermen will intercept her. She'll smile sweetly at them and tell them that Mr. Mason left the office about half an hour before, that he made arrangements to leave the office in such a way he could work on the case without interruption."

"You think they'll take her word for that?" Drake asked.

"Hell, no," Mason said grinning. "They'll come up here, though, and find the office dark."

"And be satisfied you're still in it."

"Sure they will, but they'll then get a brilliant idea, and get hold of the janitor and when the scrubwomen come in to clean up the office the newshawks will be snooping around—illegal, but they'll do it just the same. They'll want pictures and interviews."

Drake seemed dubious. "Then they'll know that you're in my office. They'll simply watch *it*."

Mason said, "We'll make them think I managed to get out through the basement."

"How?"

"There again is where you come in," Mason said, grinning. "You are going to ship a big packing case by truck. You're going to be very particular about it, and the packing case which is supposed to contain evidence is to go to the garage in my apartment house. It will be plenty heavy when you ship it. There will be a few holes bored in the lid. You'll have an operative you can trust go out to the garage, receive the package and promise to unpack it. By the time the newspaper reporters find it it will be empty."

"What makes you think they'll find it?"

"As soon as they get the idea that I may have left the

office they'll start asking questions of the janitor to find out whether I could possibly have gone out the back way. They'll also start questioning you and your office girl to find out if I'm in your office. You'll let the cat out of the bag by telling them about the packing case."

"Don't be silly," Drake said. "They've got a reporter, photographer and a plainclothes man covering the back way."

"That's fine," Mason said. "They'll all remember seeing the big box go out."

"Suppose they get suspicious and look in the box?"

"If they look in the box we'll try something else. If they don't, we'll make them think I went out that way."

"But all this isn't going to do you any good," Drake said irritably. "You're simply crucifying yourself. Figure what the papers will do when they—why, hang it, Perry, it will put your neck right in a noose. Evidence of flight is evidence of guilt."

"That's right," Mason said.

"Well, it seems to me you're playing right into Tragg's hands. You can't live in my office indefinitely, Perry."

"Of course I can't," Mason said. "That's where we use psychology. No one watches the empty barn for the stolen horse.

"Della, run out and scout the corridor. Let me know if it's clear."

Della Street nodded, opened the door, walked out into the corridor, returned and said, "It's all clear now, chief."

"Come on, Paul," Mason laughed, "you have a guest."

Drake said, wearily, "Okay, here we go again!"

Chapter 20

Mason, comfortably seated in Paul Drake's office, his feet on the edge of Drake's desk, the back of his chair propped against the wall, held a cup of coffee in his right hand, a sandwich in his left.

Paul Drake, sitting at the desk with three telephones in front of him, munched on a sandwich between incoming calls. One of the telephones rang. Drake swallowed hastily, answered the phone.

When he had finished talking and dropped the receiver into place, he said, "Well, I guess that does it, Perry."

"What happened?" Mason asked.

"That packing-case clue started the reporters off like a pack of hounds. They traced the packing case to your garage, where they found the empty case with holes bored in the lid. The newspapermen are sore and Tragg's having kittens."

"What about Goshen?"

Drake said, "At last reports Goshen was still waiting down there. He . . ."

A telephone rang.

Paul Drake picked up the receiver, placed it to his ear, said, "Okay, Drake talking . . . he did . . . Okay . . . tell you what you'd better do. You'd better be absolutely certain about that. It may be a trap. We have Goshen's address. Beat it down there, cover the place. See if Goshen actually goes home . . . Okay, call me back."

Drake dropped the receiver into place. "Goshen's gone."

"I guess that does it, Paul."

"It may be a trap," Drake pointed out. "We'll check and see if he shows up at his home. He's been waiting for hours. He'll be sore."

A telephone made noise. Drake picked up the receiver, said, "Hello, Drake talking . . . yes . . . what the hell! . . . You sure . . . ? That may be important. Hold the phone a minute—just stay on the line now. Don't let anyone disconnect you. Stay right on there."

Drake cupped his hand over the mouthpiece of the telephone and said to Mason, "They've found Hollister's car. It had been driven over a grade and wrecked."

"Any trace of Hollister?"

"No trace. Just the empty car."

"Where?" Mason asked.

"Ten and two-tenths miles above Santa del Barra on The Canyon road. Apparently it had been deliberately driven off the grade."

"What makes you think so?"

"My man's reporting. He's been in touch with the highway patrol. They discovered the car an hour ago. The car was in low gear, the ignition switch was on."

"How did they happen to find it?"

"One of the highway patrol just happened to notice very faint tracks. It was just luck he did, because the tracks were almost obliterated. They were at a wide place in the road where there's a lot of rock, and then a cliff goes straight down for something over a hundred feet into a canyon."

Mason said, "Where's your man now?"

"He's reporting from Santa del Barra."

Mason said, "Tell him to examine the car as much as the police will let him. I want to know exactly what's in it, and exactly what isn't in it."

Drake relayed instructions into the telephone, then said, "Okay, wait a minute, just hold on a second."

Once more he cupped his hand over the mouthpiece, said to Mason, "The police are going up there with a hoist.

They've phoned Tragg, and Tragg has ordered the car to be hoisted to the road. It's going to be quite a job. They'll take out a wrecking car and they'll literally have to lift the car as a dead weight up the side of the cliff."

"Okay. Tell your man to stay with the police, Paul."

Drake said into the telephone, "Stay with the police. Examine the car. Call back as soon as you have anything."

He dropped the receiver back into place, said, "Hollister didn't get very far before ditching his car."

"He got ten miles, five of it up a mountain road. Isn't that the road to Rushing Creek, Paul?"

"Good heavens, so it is!" Drake said. "Would that mean anything, Perry?"

"I don't know."

Mason started pacing the floor. "Damn it, Paul, I wish you'd get a bigger office."

"Can't afford it," Drake said. "I only need an office as headquarters. I don't have to impress clients the way you do."

Mason said, "The trouble is you have no place to walk. About the time you get started pacing the floor in this cubbyhole you run up against a wall. How the heck do you ever do any thinking?"

Drake said, "I sit in a chair when I think."

"You sure have to in this dump," Mason told him. "What are you thinking about?"

"Goshen."

"You should have let him put the finger on you and then yelled it was a frame-up," Drake said. "He'll get you sooner or later and then it'll look like hell because you ran away."

Mason kept pacing the floor.

"You can't squirm out of that situation," Drake said. "The guy's going to identify you."

"He didn't get a good look at the man's face," Mason said.

"He's had a good look at yours now. Tragg saw to that."

Mason said, "With the recovery of that car in Santa del Barra, Tragg will be tearing up there in order to see what he can find. Now Lieutenant Tragg is the brains on the homicide squad. The other boys aren't particularly smart. On the other hand, Tragg is fair, and the other chaps are inclined to take every advantage. . . . And Sergeant Holcomb would welcome a chance to knife Tragg in the back. . . . I'll tell you what let's do, Paul. Do you have an operative who's about my size and build? One whom you can trust?"

Drake looked Mason over thoughtfully, said, "Will he get into trouble?"

"Not if he does exactly as I say," Mason said.

"There's Jerry Lando. He's just about your build, and about your age."

"Can you trust him?"

"You can trust Jerry anywhere. He's been around. He's a smart cookie."

Mason said, "I remember you told me once that lots of times a camera and a flash gun would get a detective in places when no other scheme would do the work, Paul."

"That's right. Whenever anyone sees a chap carrying a press camera and a flash gun they take him for a newspaper photographer and very seldom even bother to ask questions."

"Therefore I take it you keep a camera on hand?"

"Yes."

"Okay, I want it."

"You do?"

"Yes. Also I want you to round up some good photographers. Can you get them?"

"How many?"

"Five or six."

"There's a night school in journalistic photography I could probably hire some of the advanced students."

"Okay. Get this Jerry Lando up here. Does he have a car?"

"Yes."

"Okay," Mason said. "We'll use his car. Tell him to bring a suitcase and I'll want that tan topcoat Della left here. Tell him to rush. We've got to make it fast if we pull the stunt I have in mind."

"What stunt do you have in mind?" Drake asked, reaching for the telephone.

Mason grinned, "Do *you* want to know?"

"Hell, no," Drake said hastily. He spun the dial with nervous fingers.

Chapter 21

Jerry Lando, tall, athletic, good-natured, but with a devil-may-care glint in his dark eyes, put his suitcase in the corner and said, "Okay, Mr. Drake, I have my car downstairs. It's full of gas and I'm ready for anything."

"You know Mr. Mason?" Drake asked. "Perry Mason, the lawyer?"

"How are you, Mr. Mason," Lando said, shaking hands. "I've heard a lot about you," and then grinning, he added, "and read a lot about you."

"You're going to read more," Mason told him. "We're paving the way for a story in tomorrow morning's papers."

"What do we do?" Lando asked.

Mason said, "We go to an automobile court. We pick one where the arrangement of the cabins is just the way I want it. Then you put on this tan topcoat. Let's see how it fits."

Mason held the topcoat. Lando put his arms in the sleeves, pulled it up over his shoulders.

"Just like my own coat," Lando said.

Mason said, "Paul, get your photographers. Have them bring press cameras, flash guns and lots of bulbs. How soon can you have them here?"

"Oh, give me an hour."

"I'll give you thirty minutes," Mason told him. "I'll phone in instructions. Come on, Lando, let's go."

Lando picked up his suitcase.

Mason slipped the strap of the big camera case over his shoulder.

"Have a heart, Perry," Drake pleaded. "I can't get these men on the job . . ."

"Thirty minutes is the deadline," Mason said. "Come on, Lando."

They started through the door.

Drake said hastily, "Remember you're working out of this office, Jerry. Don't let this guy get you in any trouble."

"As far as I'm concerned," Lando said, "when I'm with Mr. Mason, I'm acting under my attorney's advice."

At the elevator, the night janitor looked at Mason in open-mouthed surprise. "Why I thought you . . . Why you were supposed to have sneaked out . . ."

"Nonsense," Mason said. "I was working late."

"But you . . . you weren't in your office."

"Of course not," Mason said. "I was in conference with Paul Drake."

"Well, I'll be darned," the janitor said. "You should have seen all the trouble they made about that packing case I shipped out. Why, I'm just going to tell those boys . . ."

"Don't tell them anything for a while," Mason said. "Let them find out their own mistakes. After all, you're not responsible for what they put in the papers."

And Mason opened his wallet, selected a crisp ten-dollar bill, folded it, and slipped it into the hand of the grinning janitor.

"Your car's outside?" he asked Lando.

"Right in front of the place," Lando said.

"Okay," Mason told him. "We make a sprint for it in case anyone should be watching, but I don't think they will be."

"The place was clear as a bell when I came in," Lando said. "Everyone had cleared out."

"That's fine."

They crossed the lobby without incident, entered Lando's automobile.

"Where do we go?"

"Drive up the main highway north," Mason said. "Keep an eye out for auto courts. I want to get one that's arranged just the way I want it."

After a few miles, Mason said, "Here's a place that looks about right and I see it has a sign saying 'vacancy' so I guess we're okay."

"What accommodations do we want?"

"We want a two-room bungalow if we can get one," Mason said. "Otherwise we'll take a one-room. But it has to be at the extreme rear of the lot. Simply register as Lando and party. Give them the license number of the automobile. That's all they'll want. Do you get me?"

"I get you," Lando said.

Lando brought the car to a stop in front of the bungalow marked "Office," left the motor running and went in.

Within a couple of minutes he reappeared, accompanied by a stout woman carrying a key.

Lando beckoned, and Mason, sliding over into the driver's seat, put the car into low gear and drove slowly along until the landlady fitted a key to the door of one of the cabins in the rear.

The woman went in, followed by Lando, lights were switched on, and after a moment, Lando appeared in the doorway and nodded.

After the landlady started back to the office, Mason got out and inspected the cabin.

"Okay?" Lando asked.

"Okay," Mason said. "Now let's go telephone Paul Drake."

"There's a phone in the office."

"We don't want that," Mason said. "There's a service station down the street that has a phone. We'll use that."

"Okay," Lando said. "You want me to drive?"

"That's right. Get started and I'll tell you what you're to do while we're traveling."

Lando left the lights on, locked the door, climbed in behind the steering wheel.

Mason said, "Now, when you get Paul Drake give him the address and tell him to rush his men with the cameras out here."

"Okay."

"Then," Mason said, "wait ten minutes. Then call up police headquarters. You'll ask for Sergeant Holcomb at Homicide. You'll tell Holcomb that you're a representative of the *Blade*. Tell him that you'll give him a tip that will enable him to scoop the whole force if he'll absolutely protect you and see that the other papers don't get it."

"Suppose he says he won't?"

Mason grinned and said, "Sergeant Holcomb will promise anybody anything in order to steal a march on the other guys on the force."

"Okay, what do I tell him?"

"Tell him that your reporters have located Perry Mason out here in this auto court. Give him the number of the cabin, give him the address of the auto court, and tell him that Mason is not registered personally, but that he's with a representative of the Drake Detective Agency by the name of Lando, driving an automobile of a certain make and license number, and give him all the data. Tell him to rush Goshen out here to make an identification. Tell him your paper wants a scoop on the identification, inasmuch as you're giving him the exclusive tip."

"Okay," Lando said. "What else?"

"Then," Mason said, "we ring up the city editor at the *Blade*. Tell him you're giving *him* an exclusive tip. That if it pans out you'll call on him later for a five-spot. Tell him that Homicide is sending Goshen out here to make a surprise identification."

Lando studied Mason's guileless countenance with shrewd eyes. "This guy Holcomb knows you, doesn't he?"

"Sure he knows me," Mason said.

"Isn't that going to wreck things?"

Mason said, "Holcomb is a fiend for publicity. He's always trying to make it appear he's done something Tragg has been unable to do."

Lando said, "I still don't get it."

Mason said, "Holcomb believes in results and doesn't care how he gets them. He'll force Goshen to make an identification. Tragg wouldn't go that far."

"What I'm getting at is what Holcomb will say when he sees *you*."

Mason said, "When Holcomb drives in here he's not going to see anything."

"What do you mean?"

"Have you ever tried looking at something in the dark, just after half a dozen flash bulbs backed by silvered reflectors have popped into your eyes?"

Lando said, "I'll be damned," and his voice held admiration. He went into the service station, and started putting through calls.

Chapter 22

Mason, wearing Paul Drake's black overcoat, met the car containing Drake's men, gave them careful instructions, and assigned them to positions as carefully as a football coach working out a play.

From the highway came the sound of brakes as a car swung into the driveway leading to the auto court. The long antenna and red spotlight characterized it as a police car.

Mason said, "Okay, boys, this is it."

The car came to a stop as Drake's men converged on it. Flash bulbs blazed into brilliance, blinding the eyes of the driver and his passenger.

"Hey," Sergeant Holcomb growled, "what's the idea?"

"Just a picture for the press, Lieutenant Tragg," one of the men said.

"It ain't Lieutenant Tragg. It's Sergeant Holcomb. Be sure you get that name right now, will you? H-O-L-C-O-M-B."

"Okay, we've got it," one of the men said. "How about another picture?"

Again flashlights popped.

Mason, taking advantage of the dazzled eyes of the officer, moved forward to stand by the running board, holding the Speed Graphic in his hand. Sergeant Holcomb reached for the ignition switch, then the dash panel switch. "Is Mason really in there?"

One of the men said, "He's there. We checked the register. He's with one of Drake's men."

More flashlights blazed.

"Say, wait a minute," Holcomb protested, "you're making this look like the Fourth of July."

"Here he comes!" one of the men shouted. "He's seen the flash bulbs and he's breaking cover. He knows we've located him now."

"Here he is," Holcomb said to Goshen.

The figure which came running out of the door of the cabin, attired in a tan overcoat and holding a hat in front of his face, ran up the gravel driveway directly toward the police car.

The photographers deployed into a semicircle. Flashlights blazed into brilliance.

The figure hesitated, stopped, turned, put on the hat, and with the dignity of surrender strode back toward the cabin.

Cameramen ran along beside the figure snapping more pictures. Mason remained at the side of the police car.

"Okay," Sergeant Holcomb growled to the man at his side, "you seen him. That's him, ain't it?"

There was a silence.

"Well?" Holcomb asked.

"That's him," Goshen said.

Sergeant Holcomb chuckled, turned on the ignition, and backed the car. "Hope those pictures turn out good," he called out. "So long, boys."

As the police car drove away, Mason said to the other operatives, "All right, boys, rush back and get those pictures developed. I want each man to keep track of his own pictures he took so we can identify them."

Mason watched them drive away, then went back into the cabin and grinned to Lando.

"How did I do?" Lando asked.

"Okay," Mason said.

"It was a lot of action there for a minute. Those flashlights certainly do blind a man."

"We'll change overcoats now," Mason said. "This black

155

one isn't *quite* as good a fit. The tan one, I think, will be more comfortable. The car from the *Blade* should be here. . . . Let's see what this one is."

Headlights shone down the long driveway, as a car approached the cabin.

Lando went to the door and looked out.

A man's voice said, "We're from the *Blade*. We want to interview Mr. Mason."

"What are you talking about?" Lando asked.

"Oh, let them come in," Mason said. "If they've located me here they're entitled to an interview. We can't dodge them."

A newspaper reporter and a photographer entered the cabin.

"Hello, Mr. Mason," the reporter said.

"Hello," Mason said, grinning.

"You've been leading the cops quite a chase, haven't you?"

The photographer raised his camera, a flash blazed into brilliance.

Mason said, "I'm working on a case. I'm not letting everyone know where I am, but I'm not dodging the police. In fact, the police were here not over ten minutes ago. You want another picture? Sergeant Holcomb was out here— with Goshen."

They wanted more pictures and then asked Mason to pose in the doorway.

"And also coming out of the cabin," the photographer said.

The photographer stood in the yard. Mason opened the door, emerged from the cabin, holding his hat slightly to one side of his face.

"That's swell," the photographer said. "Looks as though you'd been trying to dodge a picture and I'd slipped around to the side and got a good one."

The reporter said, "We'd like to know more about this case, Mr. Mason, and . . ."

"Sorry, I have no comment to make on the case."

The reporter looked at his watch. "I guess that does it. Come on, Jack, let's rush these pictures back and get them developed. You say Holcomb was out here?"

"That's right. He'll give you details on the phone."

Chapter 23

At noon the next day, Mason, working casually and unconcernedly in his office, received word that Lieutenant Tragg was once more a visitor.

Tragg followed on the heels of Gertie as she made the announcement.

"Pardon me for not waiting in the outer office," Tragg said, "but you have such a habit of slipping out of doors and things, and hiding in packing cases . . . ."

Mason, a stack of morning papers on his desk, said irritably, "Damn it, Tragg, I don't know how that rumor got started."

"Well, the *Blade* certainly had a scoop," Tragg said. "Guess you had quite a time out there, didn't you?"

"Oh, so-so."

"You knew that Goshen identified you?"

"Did he?"

"Absolutely. He saw you walk and he saw you run."

Tragg settled himself comfortably in the chair. "Now look, Mason," he said, "you have a lot at stake. Don't let this two-timing little bitch get you into a position where your professional career is ruined."

"I'll try not to."

"Well, then, come clean."

Mason said, "It's just as I've told you, Tragg. You're a square shooter, but there are people in the district attorney's office who have been laying for me. They'd do anything on earth to get me."

"Well, they've got you now."

"Then let them prove it."

"They just might surprise you."

"On the other hand, I might surprise them. How did Sergeant Holcomb find out where I was last night?"

"I don't know," Tragg said. "Frankly, that was what I wanted to ask you about. Holcomb claims it was the result of some damn fine detective work. I had an idea it might— just *might,* you understand, have been the result of a tipoff."

"The *Blade* had a clean scoop. You don't suppose . . ."

"No. Holcomb's sore as hell at the *Blade*."

"Why?"

"Well, they didn't use pictures of him. They only had pictures of you giving an interview in the cottage after he'd left, and pictures of you coming out of the door trying to hold your hat in front of your face."

"I know exactly how he feels," Mason said. "Only I don't care about having my picture in the paper."

Tragg grinned. "Holcomb does."

"Is that so?"

"You know damn well it's so. He's been all over town buying papers, and he's intimating he made good on the job after I fell down."

Mason said, "That's leading with his chin."

Tragg looked long and searchingly at Perry Mason. "There's something about Holcomb's account of that thing that doesn't jibe."

"Is that particularly unusual?"

"I'm not commenting about what he says about his detective work. I'm referring to what he says about the photographers."

"Oh?"

"According to Holcomb there were photographers all over the place."

Mason lit a cigarette. "Well," he said, "Sergeant Holcomb is a trained observer. He should know."

159

"But no reporters," Tragg went on, "only photographers. Now when you stop to think of it, that's peculiar."

Mason blew smoke at the ceiling.

"Moreover, with that number of photographers every newspaper in town should have had a picture. Only the *Blade* carried the story."

"The trouble with Sergeant Holcomb," Mason observed, his eyes following the spiral of smoke which eddied up from his cigarette, "is that he hypnotizes himself, because he always wants the facts to be his way. I don't know whether you've ever noticed it, Lieutenant, but Sergeant Holcomb will get an idea, then he tries to make the facts fit that idea."

Tragg studied Mason with cautious, speculative eyes. He took a cigar from his pocket, bit off the end, lit the cigar, and said, "I'm sorry I can't promise you immunity all the way through the D.A.'s office."

"I know," Mason said.

"The way things look now," Tragg said, "they've already charged Lucille Barton with murder. They'll rush her up for a preliminary, and hold everything else in abeyance."

"Uh huh."

"Ready to close in on the others," Tragg went on, "when the situation becomes a little more clarified, as it will at the preliminary hearing. You probably know you're the one they're laying for."

"I thought they'd take me in this morning," Mason said. "In fact, I thought that was why you were coming here. I was getting my business cleaned up a bit and . . ."

"There have been complicating circumstances," Tragg said, grinning.

"What are they?"

"Hollister's automobile, for one."

"No trace of Hollister?"

"Not so far. It's only due to luck we found the car. It could have stayed there for a month or two."

"No trace of Dudley Gates?"

"Dudley Gates heard we were looking for him and telephoned us. He's in Honolulu. He'd rushed over by plane on a business deal. He tells a straightforward story, but it deepens the mystery on Hollister. Gates was planning to go with Hollister on Monday afternoon, but he had to change his plans on a few minutes' notice. He says he was supposed to go with Hollister, leaving at six o'clock Monday night, but that afternoon an urgent matter came up and he suddenly decided to fly to San Francisco, and then take a plane to Honolulu. He says he'd previously advised Hollister and Hollister had talked with him in San Francisco at about quarter of five. A check of Hollister's phone records shows that's right. He called Gates at the airport in San Francisco and had him paged. Gates said Hollister told him he was going to leave Santa del Barra within an hour."

"Very interesting," Mason said.

"That changes the whole setup. You can probably see it from the d.a.'s viewpoint."

"Anything else on Hollister's movements that afternoon?"

"At four-thirty Monday, when the housekeeper left the place, Hollister was just about ready to leave. His car was in the driveway. He told her six o'clock was the absolute deadline. We haven't been able to locate him."

"What does the housekeeper look like?"

"Not bad. About forty. She says he was playing around with Lucille and that Lucille had nicked him for furniture. Oriental rugs, an antique desk and a lot of other stuff."

"She evidently doesn't like Lucille?"

"Definitely not."

Mason nodded. "She wouldn't. Which direction was the car headed when it was run off the grade, Lieutenant—upgrade or downgrade?"

"It's hard to tell from the tracks. There's a wide place there, then the drop. The tracks are very faint and almost at

161

right angles with the road. But the car must have been driven *up* from Santa del Barra.

"Someone pulled the usual stunt of locking the car in low gear, easing it off the road over to the edge, then jerking open the hand throttle and jumping from the running board to the ground."

"Then, of course, you're looking on all of the steep turns and sharp drops farther *up* the grade?"

"*Up* the grade?"

"That's right. If someone had wanted to dispose of something in the car, and then wanted to dispose of the car, he'd find the place to run the car over the cliff, and he'd naturally dispose of the object *after* he'd located the place."

"Then it would be *down* the grade. The car must have been driven up from Santa del Barra."

"That's right. The driver would *first* spot the place to dispose of the car."

Tragg thought that over.

"But the heavy object would have to be disposed of while he still had the car."

Tragg arose hurriedly. "I'd better be going."

"Well, drop in any time," Mason said.

Tragg shook hands. "Thanks, I will."

When he had left the office Mason looked at Della Street over the circling wisp of cigarette smoke.

She said, "You virtually promised him you'd make Sergeant Holcomb wish he hadn't boasted about that identification, chief."

"Did you get that impression, Della?"

"Well, in a way, yes."

"Then Tragg must have got it."

Della frowned as she studied Mason's face. "He likes you, doesn't he?—I mean personally, not officially."

"He should," Mason said.

Chapter 24

At noon on Sunday, the ninth, Paul Drake called up Perry Mason on the unlisted telephone at the lawyer's apartment. "News for you, Perry."

"Okay," Mason said, stretching himself out luxuriously in the reclining chair, and propping the telephone to his ear, "let's have it."

"They've discovered Hollister's body."

"Where?"

"About a mile and a half *up* the grade from where Hollister's car was found."

"Well, well," Mason said, "that's very interesting."

"And he too had been shot in the head, but with a .45 caliber automatic."

"Death instantaneous I suppose?"

"Practically."

"Where was the body?"

"It had been thrown over a cliff and someone had gone down, rolled the body against the steep face of the bank and pushed dirt over it, a rather effective but very hasty burial."

Mason said, "Now get this, Paul. It's important. Was there anything unusual about that body—its position?"

"Yes. It was wrapped in canvas and trussed up with the knees pulled up across the chest, the head drawn forward, and the shoulders tied to the knees."

"Anything to show time?"

"Hollister's smashed wrist watch had stopped at 5:55. The clock on the dash of the car at 6:21. Police think Hollister must have been shot by a hitchhiker who drove the car up a side road, went through Hollister's pockets and tied him in a bundle so he could be rolled down the cliff. Then twenty-six minutes later got rid of the car. Hollister usually carried a good roll. There wasn't a dime in the pockets.

"But, of course, the police aren't at all certain. Because of his connection with Lucille Barton, they're moving very slowly."

"In other words, the police are pretty badly confused?"

"Well, they're starting to clarify the situation. They're filing a complaint charging Lucille Barton with murder, and they'll hold a preliminary hearing just as soon as they can rush it through."

"That's fine," Mason said. "How did they happen to find the body, Paul?"

"Well, Lieutenant Tragg evidently doped it out. He felt that Hollister's car had been ditched by someone who had wanted to conceal the body of the owner, that the car had been taken up the grade from Santa del Barra, then turned around and headed back down. He felt certain the body must have been ditched above the place where the car turned around, so he found a wide place in the road where it was possible to make a turn, then started looking for steep cliffs. Starting from there, he began to look for freshly dug ground and—well, he found it—incidentally he's taking a lot of kudos for some damn good detective work."

"I'm glad of that," Mason said. "He's certainly entitled to it. Didn't say anything about how he happened to get that hunch, did he, Paul?"

"No, it was just clever detective work on his part."

"I see," Mason said. "And what else did they find other than the body?"

"Nothing. Isn't that enough?"

"No."

"What do you mean?"

"If Hollister was starting out on a trip, he'd have had . . ."

"Oh, you mean baggage?"

"Yes."

Drake was silent for a few seconds, then said, "It's a good point, Perry. I don't think there was any."

"Well, thanks a lot for calling, Paul. I don't think they'll try to arrest anyone else until after Lucille Barton's preliminary. You should see a lot of action there, Paul."

"Heaven help us both if I don't," Drake said wearily as he hung up the telephone.

Chapter 25

Perry Mason, surveying the crowded courtroom, walked over to engage in a whispered conference with Paul Drake and Della Street.

"Hamilton Burger, the district attorney, is going to take charge of the preliminary personally," Mason said in a low voice. "That means he's gunning for me. He . . ."

The door from the judge's chambers opened and Judge Osborn walked into the courtroom and took his place on the bench.

"People versus Lucille Barton," he said. "This is the time fixed for the preliminary hearing. Are you ready, gentlemen?"

Hamilton Burger, big, ponderous, dignified, built like some huge bear, was on his feet, his voice suave, plausible, his manner radiating a synthetic impartiality, which was deadly in its effect on jurors.

"Your Honor," he said, "we are ready. Now I am going to state to the Court frankly that the death of Hartwell L. Pitkin is to some extent shrouded in mystery, but at this preliminary hearing it is only necessary for us to show that a crime was committed and to show that there is reasonable cause to believe the defendant committed that crime.

"I am very frank to state to Your Honor that I am hoping the evidence in this case will clear up some elements of the mystery and I will further add that before the case is done, we will quite probably ask for a warrant to be issued for at least one other person."

And Hamilton Burger turned meaningly toward Perry Mason.

"We're quite ready to proceed, Your Honor," Mason said. "All we ask is an opportunity to meet the issues and cross-examine the People's witnesses."

"I may say," Hamilton Burger snapped, "that our investigation in this case has been somewhat handicapped by the fact that counsel for the defendant has apparently been active in this case from its inception, *even before* the murder of Hartwell Pitkin."

"Go on with your proof," Mason said. "Don't try to prejudice the Court."

"I'm not trying to prejudice the Court," Burger snapped, his voice and manner showing the seething anger which raged within him. "I'm merely trying to explain to the Court that we have been handicapped in this case from its inception. Our witnesses have been unable to make proper identifications because of tactics used by counsel for the defense."

"What tactics?" Mason asked in surprise.

"Refusing to stand up so that a witness could identify you, for one thing," Burger said, raising his voice so that the volume of sound reverberated through the courtroom. "And following that, Your Honor, counsel permitted himself to be secreted in a packing case so that he could be spirited out of his office building through the freight exit in order to thwart the attempts of . . ."

"That's not true," Mason said cheerfully.

"Gentlemen, gentlemen," Judge Osborn said. "This is neither the time nor the place for such a discussion. If you have evidence, Mr. District Attorney, put it on."

"He hasn't any, and he can't get any," Mason said.

"Don't tell me I haven't and can't!" Burger shouted, his face darkening. "I'll show you whether or not I have any such evidence. You give me half a chance, and I'll prove that you were spirited out of your office building in a packing case so a witness by the name of Carl Evert Goshen couldn't identify you; that you then went to the Sleepwell

Auto Court with a bodyguard, where you tried to hide until the witness found you and made an absolute identification."

"Go ahead and prove it," Mason said.

"And the minute I try to prove *that* in *this* case you'll start objecting that it's not within the issues," Burger said contemptuously. "*Our* hands are tied, and you know it."

Mason said, "If you have witnesses who can prove any such thing, I won't make a single objection."

"Come, come, gentlemen," Judge Osborn said. "The Court has to be considered in this matter. We have a crowded calendar. This is merely a preliminary examination and . . ."

"If Your Honor will permit me to take up counsel's offer," Hamilton Burger said, "I'll convince the Court that the time consumed by putting on that evidence is the most important time Your Honor has ever spent on the bench. I'll blast the subterfuge of this scheming attorney wide open. I'll show him in his true colors. I'll . . ."

Judge Osborn's gavel banged on the desk. "You'll refrain from these insulting personalities, Mr. District Attorney."

"I beg the Court's pardon," Burger said, controlling himself with difficulty. "I have been led to lose some measure of my self-control by the tactics I've encountered in this case. Counsel has made an offer. He's made it publicly. I don't think he dares to stand by that offer, but I would like to . . ."

"You go ahead and put on your proof," Judge Osborn said. "The Court will not permit its time to be taken up with extraneous matters, but I think you know this Court well enough to know that any legitimate attempt to get at the truth will be welcome."

"Very well," Hamilton Burger sneered. "Counsel has stated he won't object. I'll lay the preliminary proof of the *corpus delicti* by showing that Hartwell L. Pitkin was employed by Stephen Argyle as a chauffeur and butler; that on the fifth of this month he was murdered, having been shot with a Smith and Wesson revolver, number S65088. I'll call Lieutenant Tragg as a witness."

Tragg took the witness stand, testified to his official connection with the police and the fact that he was on the homicide squad; that on the fifth he had been called to a garage in the back of an apartment house at number 719 South Gondola; that there he had found the body of Hartwell L. Pitkin.

Tragg then went on to describe the body, the manner in which it had been found, and what had been done.

"There was a gun lying near the right hand of the body?" Burger asked.

"That's right," Tragg said. "It was a .38 caliber Smith and Wesson number S65088. An attempt had been made to remove all the numbers but one number had been overlooked and was still intact. The cylinder contained five loaded shells and one empty shell."

"Is this the weapon?" Burger asked, producing the gun.

"It is, yes, sir."

"I ask that it be marked for identification, Your Honor."

"Very well. It will be so marked."

"Now, Lieutenant, you say this gun was found near the body?"

"Yes, sir, but a paraffin test showed the decedent had not fired a gun. Also there had been an extensive hemorrhage from a wound in the head. We found this gun lying *on top of the pool of blood*. There was no blood on the gun except on the *under* side. There were blood spatters on the hand of the decedent. There were no spatters on the gun and no fingerprints whatever on the outside of the gun."

"How about the inside of the gun?" Burger asked.

"On the *inside* of the gun," Tragg said, "we found a fingerprint which was subsequently identified as being a print of a man's right index finger."

"Whose finger?" Burger asked.

"Perry Mason's finger," Tragg said.

"You have those fingerprints here?"

"I have them here."

"Your Honor," Burger said apologetically, "this is perhaps the wrong way to introduce this evidence. I should technically have produced a photograph of the fingerprint and then prints of Mr. Mason's fingers and compared them, but in view of the fact that there can't be any question about the identification of the print, and in view of . . ."

"I'm not going to object," Mason interrupted. "Go right ahead. Handle it any way you want to, Mr. District Attorney."

"Thank you," Burger said sarcastically. "Now, Lieutenant Tragg, if you have those fingerprints we'll introduce them in evidence. People's Exhibit A, the fingerprint that was found on the inside of the gun. People's Exhibit B, a print that was taken from Mr. Mason's right index finger. Now, will you describe the circumstances under which you took that fingerprint of Mr. Mason's right index finger?"

Tragg said, "That was on Thursday, the sixth. I went to Mr. Mason's office with a Mr. Goshen . . ."

"His full name?"

"Carl Evert Goshen."

"You had there some conversation with Mr. Mason?"

"Isn't this entirely outside of the issues, Mr. District Attorney?"

"I think I can connect it up," Burger said. "Mr. Mason is not objecting."

"I understand Mr. Mason's position. However, I don't care to hear a lot of extraneous or hearsay evidence."

"This isn't hearsay. This gets right down to the gist of the case."

"All right, go ahead."

Burger said, "Mr. Goshen was there with you, Lieutenant Tragg. Who else?"

"The defendant in the case, Lucille Barton, a gentleman by the name of Arthur Colson, who had apparently been interested in the purchase of the gun, and a plainclothes officer."

"Mr. Mason permitted you to take his fingerprints?"

"Yes."

"Did he make any comment about his fingerprint being on the inside of the gun?"

"He admitted that he had used a key which he said he had received in the mail to enter the apartment of Lucille Barton on the day of the murder . . ."

"Come, come, gentlemen," Judge Osborn interrupted. "Despite the fact that there isn't any objection from the attorney for the defense, I feel that . . ."

"But he admitted seeing the gun in the defendant's apartment," Burger said.

"*A* gun," Mason corrected.

"Well, *a* gun similar to this gun," Burger retorted. "That certainly is significant and it's relevant."

"Yes, I suppose so," Judge Osborn said. "Go right ahead."

Lieutenant Tragg said, "At that time I pointed out to Mr. Mason that Mr. Goshen was a witness who had seen two people at the garage where the body was found at about the time the murder must have been committed. One of these persons Goshen had previously identified as the defendant. She was accompanied by a man who answered the description of Mr. Perry Mason. I asked Mr. Mason to stand up so that Mr. Goshen could see if he were the same person. Mr. Mason refused to do so."

"You mean he refused to get up?" Mr. Burger said, his voice for dramatic emphasis showing a synthetic incredulity. "You mean that Mr. Mason, an attorney at law, refused to let a witness look at him to see if he could be identified as a man who had accompanied . . ."

"I think that question's argumentative and has already been asked and answered in effect," Judge Osborn said. "The court is going to try to keep this examination somewhere within the limits of the legal rules. It is, of course, a peculiar situation where an attorney for the defense refuses to object." And Judge Osborn frowned disapprovingly at Perry Mason.

"Your Honor," Mason said, "quite obviously the district attorney is preparing to attack my reputation by insinuation and innuendo. He knows, of course, that the press is represented at this hearing. I am fully aware that by pretending to be balked by technical objections on my part he can leave the impression that I am fighting to suppress the real facts. Therefore, I am throwing the doors wide open. If he has any facts, I want them brought out."

"Well," Judge Osborn said, "I guess, on second thought, I can appreciate your position, Mr. Mason. However, of course, the Court can't be used as a place for trying personalities."

"These aren't personalities, Your Honor," Hamilton Burger said. "This gets right down to the meat of the situation."

"All right, go ahead, start carving," Judge Osborn said.

"Now, then, did you subsequently make an attempt to have Mr. Mason identified by Mr. Goshen?"

"I most certainly did."

"What did you do?"

"I had Mr. Goshen in my car with me, waiting in front of the exit of Mr. Mason's office building. I was working in cooperation with reporters who were also covering the freight exit of the building and who were prepared to signal me in the event Mr. Mason left the building by that entrance."

"And what did Mr. Mason do?"

Tragg grinned and said, "He had himself put in a packing case and shipped out of the back door as merchandise."

There was a ripple of merriment through the courtroom.

"Did Goshen subsequently identify Mr. Mason?"

"I wasn't there at the time," Tragg said. "One of my

associates, Sergeant Holcomb, was there when that happened."

"Cross-examine," Burger said triumphantly.

Mason said smilingly, "How do *you* know that I left the building in a packing case, Lieutenant?"

"Well, now," Tragg said hurriedly, "perhaps I should correct that. As a matter of fact, I only knew it from what I read in the papers and what I was told. I didn't *see* you leave the building in the packing case. If I had . . ." He broke off and grinned.

"Did you talk with anyone who saw me in that packing case, Lieutenant?"

"No, sir."

"You have any reason to believe I was in that packing case?"

"Yes, sir."

"What makes you think so?"

"It was the only way you could have got out of the building without having been observed."

"Permit me to correct you, Lieutenant. You probably don't realize it, but as a matter of fact I was in Paul Drake's office until late that evening, until long after the packing case had been shipped. If you had talked with the janitor of the building you would have found that I left and went down in the elevator with him, accompanied by one of Paul Drake's men, a Mr. Jerry Lando, a man, incidentally, who is here in court and who can be questioned by you at any time."

Tragg's face showed surprise. "You mean . . ."

"I mean exactly what I say, Lieutenant. I'd suggest that you have a talk with Mr. Lando before you make any more accusations based on hearsay. Now, thank you very much, Lieutenant Tragg. I have no further questions on cross-examination."

Tragg and Burger exchanged glances. Tragg stepped down from the witness stand, turned when he was halfway across the courtroom and said, "Where is this Jerry Lando?"

"Right here," Jerry Lando said, standing up.

"Never mind," Hamilton Burger said, hiding embarrassment behind a new belligerency. "I'll call Sergeant Holcomb to the witness stand and we'll clear *that* matter up very rapidly."

Sergeant Holcomb came striding forward, raised his hand, took the oath, and with a satisfied anticipatory grin, settled himself in the witness chair.

Hamilton Burger asked a few preliminary questions as to name, age, residence, occupation, and then plunged into the evidence. "Sergeant, where were you on the evening of the sixth—that was Thursday, you'll remember."

"I remember," Sergeant Holcomb grinned. "I located Perry Mason at the Sleepwell Auto Court and got a witness by the name of Carl Goshen to accompany me. We went out to make an identification. We made it."

Sergeant Holcomb grinned gleefully as he thought over the events of the evening.

"What happened while you were there and in your presence?" Burger asked.

"Well, we drove into the auto court and in some way the word got around to newspapers. A bunch of newspaper photographers were out there. They took pictures of us when we drove in. They did that before I could stop them."

"And then what happened?"

"Well, when the flash bulbs started popping, Mason, who was in Cabin Number 6, evidently accompanied by this Jerry Lando because Jerry Lando had signed the register and given the license number of his car, well, Mr. Mason came running out, and when he saw all the newspaper photographers he put his hat up in front of his face to try and keep them from getting his picture; but they started shooting flash bulbs anyway. Then he saw he was trapped, so he turned around and walked back to the cabin."

174

"Did you follow him into the cabin?"

"No, sir."

"Why not?"

Sergeant Holcomb grinned and said, "Because it wasn't necessary. I'd done all I wanted to do. The witness Goshen, who was with me, had seen Mason come out of the cabin, had seen him walk and run, had seen his size and build, and he identified him absolutely as the man he'd seen in front of that garage about the time the murder was being committed. He'd previously identified the defendant, Lucille Barton."

"This is a highly irregular manner of receiving evidence," Judge Osborn snapped. "The witness Goshen should speak for himself."

"He will," Hamilton Burger promised. "I'm simply taking up Mason's challenge and proving that I had the evidence I said I had. The Court will observe that it has only taken some twenty minutes of the Court's time."

"Very well," Judge Osborn said. "It is of course a most unusual situation, the defendant's counsel permitting all this hearsay evidence without objection."

Sergeant Holcomb said, "It isn't hearsay, Your Honor. I was sitting right there when Goshen made the identification. I heard what he said."

"That's *exactly* what is meant by hearsay," Judge Osborn said. "You don't know whether the man at the garage was Perry Mason. *You* only know what the witness said. The witness should speak for himself."

"Well, he will," Hamilton Burger interposed hastily. "He'll be my next witness, if the Court please."

"Very well, finish with this witness," Judge Osborn said.

"I'm finished with him now," Burger announced triumphantly.

Sergeant Holcomb started to leave the stand.

"Just a minute," Mason said. "I want to ask you a few questions about that identification at the Sleepwell Auto Court, Sergeant. Now, *you've* known me for some time?"

"Yes, sir."

"You recognized me when I ran out of the cabin and you said to Goshen, "There he is. There's Mason now,' or words to that effect?"

"I don't think I had to say anything like that. He recognized you as soon as he saw you."

"You may not have thought you *had* to say it, but you *did* say it."

"I may have."

"The man who ran out had his hat in front of his face?"

"*You* had *your* hat in front of *your* face, trying to keep people from taking *your* picture."

"Then this man turned his back and walked back to the cabin?"

"That's right. That's exactly what *you* did."

"How far did the man run from the cabin before he turned around and ran back?"

"Oh, some thirty or forty feet."

"There were several newspaper photographers there?"

"Yes, sir."

"How do you know they were newspaper photographers?"

"Well, I . . . I . . ."

"In other words, you just *assumed* they must have been newspaper photographers, is that right?"

Holcomb said angrily and sarcastically, "That's right. I'm just a dumb cop, but when a newspaper gives me a tip, when I see a bunch of guys carrying press cameras with flash bulbs fixed in reflectors, I just get credulous enough to think they're newspaper men. It's careless of me!"

"Oh, so you had a tip from a newspaper?"

"Well, I used methods of my own."

"How did you know I was there at this auto court?"

Holcomb grinned. "A little bird told me."

"And when you got there, there were some half dozen photographers there?"

"Right."

"Some of them took your picture?"

"Yes, sir."

"Can you remember any of them? Would you know them if you saw them again?"

"Why, I don't know," Sergeant Holcomb said. "I . . ."

"If you can identify the man you saw running out of the cabin, why couldn't you identify some of the photographers?"

"Well, as a matter of fact, that's sort of hard to do when those flash bulbs are popping in your eyes. I . . ."

"Oh, so you were dazzled by flash bulbs?" Mason said.

"Not enough so I couldn't recognize *you*," Sergeant Holcomb shouted.

"I see," Mason said, smiling. "The flash bulbs dazzled you so you couldn't see any of the other men, but they didn't dazzle you enough so you couldn't see me."

"I didn't say that."

"Well, how about those other men—can you describe them?"

"I can describe some of them."

"Well, go ahead."

"Well," Sergeant Holcomb said, "there was a photographer right next to me, the man who came up and took my picture at the first. He was wearing a black overcoat."

"About how old?"

"I couldn't tell how old he was from looking at him out of the corner of my eye. He was a youngish man."

"About how tall?"

"Oh . . . fairly tall, perhaps about as tall as you are."

"About how heavy?"

Holcomb looked Mason over thoughtfully and said, "Somewhat your build."

"Did you talk with this man?"

"I don't think so. I tell you I was looking at you when you ran out of the cabin. I had my headlights on and you ran right into those headlights and put up your hat to shield your face, and—acted like a shyster lawyer caught in a web of his own trickery, and . . ."

"That will do!" Judge Osborn shouted, pounding with his gavel. "That is absolutely uncalled for, Sergeant Holcomb! You know better than that."

Sergeant Holcomb said angrily, "Well, he's trying to insinuate I couldn't see him."

"Nevertheless, these personalities are uncalled for. Now, while you're in court, Sergeant, you confine yourself to answering questions. Otherwise the Court is going to have to take some disciplinary action. Do you understand?"

"Yes, sir," Sergeant Holcomb said sullenly.

"Now, you say this man who was standing next to you took your picture as you drove up?" Mason asked.

"That's right."

"What were you doing when the picture was taken? Do you remember?"

"I remember exactly," Sergeant Holcomb said. "I was leaning forward to turn off the ignition, and also the switch on the dashboard which controlled the dash and panel lights, so this man Goshen could get a better view; that is, so he could look through the windshield without having lights in his eyes."

Mason said, "I'll show you a photograph, Sergeant Holcomb, and ask you if that's the photograph which was taken of you at that moment by this photographer who was standing beside your car. You'll notice it shows the witness Goshen sitting in the car and you're leaning forward to . . ."

"That's the picture," Sergeant Holcomb said. "That's the one that was taken at that moment."

"That was the only time you leaned forward, when you turned off the ignition and the dash and panel lights?"

"That's right. That's the picture that was taken by that photographer who was standing right next to me."

"And that flashlight didn't dazzle your eyes?"

"Not mine," Sergeant Holcomb said. "My eyes are good. I'm accustomed to driving a lot at night and headlights don't bother me. I can look right past a glare and . . . No, sir, those flashlights didn't bother me at all. They didn't keep me from seeing everything that was going on."

"Now, at about that time," Mason said, "there was another photographer directly in front of the automobile who took a photograph right through the windshield, wasn't there?"

"I believe so, yes, but you can't mix me up by making the claim that those flashlight bulbs blinded us, because they didn't."

"No, no," Mason said, "I'm not making that claim. I'm simply trying to identify the order in which the photographs were taken. Now, here is another photograph which shows you leaning forward in the automobile and apparently was taken immediately before, or immediately after the photographer who was on your left had taken his picture. This, however, is taken from the front of the car, looking through the windshield."

"That's right," Sergeant Holcomb said. "That's the picture."

"That picture shows you, shows Mr. Goshen, and shows the photographer who had just taken this first picture. Is that right?"

"That's right."

"All right," Mason said. "Let's have these photographs marked for identification as Defendant's Exhibit One and Defendant's Exhibit Two."

The clerk marked the photographs.

"Now, then," Mason said, "at about that time, there were other photographers taking pictures of the man who ran out of the cabin?"

"You hadn't run out of the cabin then," Sergeant Holcomb said. "You can't trap me that way, Mr. Mason. The photographers all clustered around and took our pictures when I first drove up. Then the flashing of those bulbs made you realize something was wrong. You broke cover and came dashing out of that cabin just like a rabbit breaking cover and running away. When you saw all that gang in front of you, you turned around and scuttled right back into the cabin, but not until Goshen had had plenty of opportunity to identify you."

"And as that figure came running out, the photographers took pictures of him?"

"That's right, pictures of *you*."

"Holding his hat up?"

"That's right, holding *your* hat up."

"Now, then," Mason said, "I'll show you a photograph which I would like to have marked for identification as Defendant's Exhibit Number Three, and which shows a figure running out from this cabin with a hat in front of his face."

"That's the one," Sergeant Holcomb said. "That's a good picture. That shows *you* running out with a hat up in front of *your* face."

"Exactly," Mason said. "We'll have that as Defendant's Exhibit for identification Number Three. Now, I'll show you Defendant's Exhibit for identification Number Four, Sergeant Holcomb, and you will notice that that shows the running man, but slightly from a side view. It also shows the photographer who has just taken picture Number Three."

Holcomb studied the picture, said, "That's right. That seems to be the way the picture was taken. That's it, all right."

"But," Mason said, "you will notice that in this picture which is marked Number Four for identification, Sergeant, the angle of the camera was a little to one side so that the features of the man are a little more plainly visible than this photograph Number Three."

"Yes, I guess they are," Holcomb admitted.

"Now, then," Mason said, "I'll show you a photograph,

Exhibit Number Five, which shows the running figure with the hat held in front of his face, and also shows the photographers who took pictures Three and Four."

"That's right," Sergeant Holcomb said mechanically.

"That's right?"

"That's right."

"Better take another look at that picture," Mason said. "You can see the man's profile in it quite clearly. Do you think that is my picture, Sergeant?"

Sergeant Holcomb suddenly grabbed at the picture, said, "Wait a minute. I'd better get my glasses on here." He reached in his pocket, adjusted spectacles, studied the picture, said suddenly, "No, this isn't you. There's some sort of a flimflam work here! *That's* another man!"

"Exactly," Mason said. "Now, if you will look at the photograph marked for identification as Exhibit Number Two, Sergeant, and look at the man standing with the camera just to the side of your automobile, the man who took picture Number One, just as you were leaning forward, you may recognize the features of that man."

"Just a minute—just a minute," Hamilton Burger said. "I want to see those pictures. What's happening here?"

"Come up and take a look at them," Mason invited.

Sergeant Holcomb, studying the picture, said suddenly, "That isn't right. This is fake photography."

Mason smiled. "What makes you think it's fake photography, Sergeant?"

"Because that isn't the way it happened. This is another one of your slick flimflams."

Mason said, "Better be careful with your accusations, Sergeant. We have six reputable witnesses to testify as to what happened there. Now, do you see any signs on that photograph that indicate it's a fake photograph?"

"I don't know enough about photography to tell," Sergeant Holcomb said.

"Then how do you know it's a fake?"

"Because it isn't—it isn't the way things happened."

"Oh, yes it is," Mason said. "Now, as a matter of fact, Sergeant, let's remember you're under oath here. When you first drove up to that cabin, photographers came and clustered around the automobile and took a whole series of flashlight pictures of you, didn't they?"

"I've told you they did."

"And let's remember our oath, now," Mason said. "Isn't it a fact, Sergeant, that the effect of those flashlights blinded your eyes so that you were temporarily incapable of seeing clearly—particularly objects in the semidarkness on the side of the car?"

"Well, I tell you I wasn't looking at those objects. I was looking at that house because right at that time the door popped open and . . . and . . ."

"Go on," Mason said, smiling, "and remember you're under oath, Sergeant, and that there are six reputable witnesses to testify what took place there."

"Well," Sergeant Holcomb said lamely, "the door popped open and this running man came out."

"Holding his hat in front of his face?"

"Yes."

"So you couldn't see his face?"

"Well, I . . ."

"Did you or didn't you see his face?" Mason asked.

"Well, I didn't see his face, no."

"Then how could you tell who he was?"

"Well, I—I thought I recognized him by his walk and the way he ran, and . . . Well, I'd been told Perry Mason was hiding in that cabin, and . . ."

"Exactly," Mason said. "You *expected* me to run out. Therefore, when a figure ran out and acted as you expected I might act under the circumstances you . . ."

"Oh, Your Honor, I object to this," Hamilton Burger said. "This is incompetent, irrelevent and immaterial. It's argumentative. It's not proper cross-examination."

"Well, well," Mason said, smiling. "Look who's objecting now!"

"I think the pictures speak for themselves," Judge Osborn said.

"Well, if the Court please," Hamilton Burger announced, "this is manifestly an unfair advantage to take of a witness. It is quite on a par with the trickery for which counsel is noted. It's . . ."

"Sure, it's trickery," Mason said, "but it's a trickery which wouldn't confuse an honest witness. As a matter of fact, Sergeant Holcomb's eyes were blinded by those flash bulbs just as I expected they'd be. He isn't frank enough nor honest enough to admit it, but he is sitting here under oath on this witness stand and he's going to tell the truth or he's going to be guilty of perjury. There are six witnesses who took these pictures and will identify them. Now, I want to know from Sergeant Holcomb right here and now and on cross-examination whether *I* was the person who ran out of that cabin, or whether *I* was the person standing within four feet of his left elbow holding a camera focused on his face and taking a flashlight picture. Now which was it, Sergeant?"

Sergeant Holcomb's face was a picture of dismay.

"Oh, Your Honor," Hamilton Burger said, "that's an unfair question. That . . ."

"Objection is overruled," Judge Osborn snapped. "Let the witness answer the question."

"Which was it?" Mason asked, grinning cheerfully at the discomfited officer. "And remember we have both photographs and photographers to refute any false testimony."

"I don't know," Sergeant Holcomb blurted.

"Thank you," Mason said. "That concludes my cross-examination, Sergeant. And now I believe, Mr. District Attorney, you said you wanted to put Mr. Goshen on the stand as your next witness. Put him on. Let's hear what Mr. Goshen has to say."

Hamilton Burger said, "Your Honor, I dislike these personalities . . ."

"Counsel is merely repeating a promise which you made," Judge Osborn said, fighting back a smile. "Of course, I will admit that his manner is perhaps more dramatic than the situation calls for, but . . . in any event, proceed with your case, Mr. Burger."

Hamilton Burger said, "I would like to ask the Court at this time for a five-minute recess. I would like to confer briefly with one of my associates. This situation has taken me somewhat by surprise."

"And I submit, Your Honor," Mason said, "that counsel has repeatedly promised to put the witness Goshen on the stand. I'd like to have him go on the stand now before there's been any opportunity to coach him."

"I resent that!" Burger shouted. "I have no intention of coaching the witness. He doesn't need any coaching."

"Put him on then," Mason challenged.

"I have made a motion for a five-minute recess."

"I've opposed it," Mason said.

"The motion is denied," Judge Osborn ruled. "The Court sees no reason for a recess at this time."

"Very well, then, I'll call Roscoe R. Hansom to the stand."

"I thought you were going to call Goshen," Mason said.

"I don't have to follow your instructions or the instructions of anyone else in putting on my case. I can put it on any way I please!" Burger shouted.

Mason said, "You were hurling challenges at me a few moments ago, Mr. District Attorney, now I'll hurl one right back at you. I *dare* you to put Mr. Goshen on the stand *as you promised*, and before you've had an opportunity to talk with him about this new development."

Hamilton Burger sullenly said, "I asked for Roscoe R. Hansom. Mr. Hansom, will you come forward please?"

Mason grinned.

Judge Osborn clamped his lips together in a firm, thin line.

Hansom identified himself as the proprietor of the Rushing Creek Mercantile Company, told of selling the gun, and of the general description of the man who had purchased the gun. He then produced the gun register, and the signature of the man who had signed for that gun on the register. The gun, which had been previously marked for identification, was received in evidence as People's Exhibit C.

"Have you subsequently seen that man?" Burger asked.

"Yes, sir."

"Who was he?"

"His name is Arthur Colson. I saw him at your office on the morning of the sixth."

"Cross-examine," Burger snapped.

"No questions," Mason said, gleefully. "Do you want to call Mr. Goshen now?"

"Your Honor," Burger said, "I resent this continual nagging by counsel."

"You've invited it," Judge Osborn said.

"Nevertheless, Your Honor, I feel that it is improper."

"It is improper," the Court said. "However, I can tell you this much, Mr. District Attorney. You can stall around if you want to. You've a perfect right to put on your case in any way that you see fit. But when it comes to a showdown, your proof is going to be addressed to the discretion of the Court. Now I take it there's a matter of identification of this defendant by the witness, Goshen, which is material. Very material to your case."

"Yes, Your Honor."

"And you promised; in fact, you threatened; I may say you bragged, that you were going to put this witness on the stand in order to prove certain statements you made in your opening address to the Court. Now the judge of this Court wasn't born yesterday, and I know that if you stall matters along until the Court takes its usual adjournment for recess that there's a reason for doing it. And in the mind of the Court such tactics are going to greatly weaken the testimony of the witness Goshen. Now that's plain talk, Mr. District Attorney, but it's because of a situation which you yourself invited. I'm speaking my mind. There's no jury here. This is a preliminary hearing. It's a matter addressed entirely to the discretion of the Court and that's the way the Court feels about it. Now proceed with your case."

Hamilton Burger cleared his throat, stood for a moment undecided, then blurted out, "Carl Evert Goshen, take the stand."

Goshen took the witness stand, and, after the preliminary questions, stated that he lived next door to the apartment house at 719 South Gondola. He had occasion to remember the evening of the fifth and in particular was annoyed by an automobile which had sputtered and backfired with a series of explosions which indicated the carburetor or the timing, or both, were badly out of adjustment.

"What did you do?" Burger asked.

"I opened the window, intending to call to the people across the way, asking them to shut off that motor, or do something about it," Goshen said.

"Did you do so?"

"No, sir, I didn't."

"Why?"

"Because they shut off the motor at right about that time."

"And did you see the car and the people?"

"Yes, sir."

"How far away were they?"

"Well, they were across an alley which leads to the garage. Oh, I'd say they were perhaps seventy-five feet."

"Were the figures illuminated?"

"Well, sir, the headlights were on on the automobile and I could see these figures moving around. They were looking in the garage and—well, I saw their backs and saw how they were dressed."

"Now can you describe those figures?"

"Yes, sir. One of them was Lucille Barton, the defendant in this case. She was wearing a plaid coat and a black hat with a little red feather. A hat that was close-fitting and slanted down on her head over to the right. She had those same clothes on when the police showed her to me."

"And the other figure?"

"Well, now," Goshen said, crossing his legs and running his hand over the top of his partially bald head, "now you've got me guessing."

The courtroom broke into laughter.

Hamilton Burger frowned, and said, "You have your two eyes, don't you know what you saw?"

Goshen rubbed his head, "And I've got my two ears, and I know what I've just heard."

Even Judge Osborn joined in the laughter which rocked the courtroom.

When order had been restored, Burger said, sullenly, "Well, tell us what you saw as best you can."

"Well, I saw a tall man. I never did see his face. He was a tall, athletic looking fellow, apparently sort of young, from the way he moved, not real young, but moving around sort of easy like. He took long strides, had long legs, and he was wearing a gray hat and a tan overcoat."

"Have you ever seen that man again? Can you identify him?"

"Well, now," Goshen said, hesitating and rubbing his hand over his head, "I just don't rightly know."

The courtroom tittered and Judge Osborn pounded it to silence.

"But you can positively identify the defendant?" Hamilton Burger asked.

"Objected to as leading and suggestive, assuming a fact not in evidence, argumentative, and putting words in the mouth of the defendant," Mason said.

"The objection is sustained."

"Well," Hamilton Burger said, "you definitely know how she was dressed?"

"Yes, sir."

"And her height, weight, age, and general build?"

"Yes, sir."

"And the man. Was he about the same height as anyone you are now looking at?"

"Objected to as leading and suggestive."

"Objection sustained."

"Well, how can you describe him?"

"Objected to as already asked and answered."

"Objection sustained."

"Cross-examine," Hamilton Burger snapped, with exasperation.

Mason said, "You *thought* you saw that same person again, didn't you?"

"I certainly thought I did, Mr. Mason, yes, sir. It was just the way Sergeant Holcomb has described it."

"In other words, the figure you saw at the garage that night was a man of just about the same height, build, and wearing about the same colored garments as the man you saw emerging from the auto court?"

"That's right."

"But you never did see the man's face?"

"No, sir."

"When you saw him at the garage you saw only his back?"

"Yes, sir."

"So all you know is that you saw a rather tall man with a tan-colored topcoat and a gray hat."

"Yes, sir."

"And any tall man of approximately the same build, wearing those garments, would look just about the same to you as the man you saw at that time?"

"Well, I . . . no I don't think so. I think probably I could identify him."

Mason said, "You *did* identify him, didn't you?"

"What do you mean?"

"You heard the Sergeant's testimony that you pointed out the man who ran out of that cabin."

"Well, I guess I made a mistake there," Goshen admitted, gulping in embarrassment.

"What makes you think you made a mistake?"

"Well, that man evidently was someone who had been planted there."

"What makes you think you made a mistake?"

"Well . . . my gosh, Mr. Mason, you've just proved it wasn't you."

"In other words," Mason said, "you had been told that the man you had seen at the garage was none other than Perry Mason?"

"Well, that's what the police seemed to think."

"You'd been told that?"

"Yes."

"And when you saw that man run out of the cabin you said to Sergeant Holcomb, 'that's the man,' didn't you?"

"Well, I guess I did."

"And you saw that figure running toward the headlights of an automobile, and you saw it turn around and run back?"

"Yes, sir."

"You saw it as plainly as you saw the figure that you were looking at across the alley?"

"Well, I . . . as a matter of fact, those flashlights popping in my eyes certainly did make everything seem all sort of black to me, sort of hard to look at."

"But you saw the figure well enough so that you were willing to identify him?"

"Well, yes."

"And did identify him?"

"Yes."

"And now think you were mistaken?"

"Well, I guess I must have been."

"Simply because the figure was not that of the man police had told you you must have seen at the garage, is that right?"

"Well . . . I . . . I just don't rightly know how to say it, Mr. Mason, but I guess I walked into a trap and . . . and I guess," he added ruefully, "I've got my fingers caught."

Even Judge Osborn smiled.

"And this woman whom you saw across the alley was with a man?"

"Yes."

"And you saw her at the same time and place as the man?"

"Yes, sir."

"Under the same conditions?"

"Yes, sir."

"And if you can't identify the man, how do you expect to identify the woman?"

"Well—well, I really could have identified that man if I hadn't made a mistake."

"You did identify a man?"

"Yes."

"And now you think it was the wrong man?"

"It must have been."

"And you saw the woman there at the garage no more distinctly than you saw the man."

"Well, no."

"Thank you," Mason said. "That's all."

"And *now*," Judge Osborn said, cocking a stern eye at Hamilton Burger, "the Court will take a ten-minute recess."

Chapter 26

As soon as Judge Osborn had left the bench, Lucille Barton turned to Perry Mason, placed her gloved hand over his wrist, squeezed so hard the leather of the glove stretched taut over her knuckles.

"Mr. Mason, you're wonderful!" she whispered.

Mason said, "This is just the opening round, Lucille, we've shaken the witness in his identification of me; but don't overlook the fact that his identification of you will stand up unless we can find some way of showing you weren't there."

"Yes, that's so," she admitted in a whisper.

"And," Mason said, "the gun with which Pitkin was killed was a gun that quite evidently had been given you by Arthur Colson. And incidentally, Ross Hollister was also murdered, and you had twenty thousand dollars insurance on Hollister's life."

"But, Mr. Mason, can't you understand? I loved Ross. His death is a great blow to me. We were going to be married. He represented security, affection, a home, everything a woman wants."

"Unless, perhaps, she happened to have been in love with Arthur Colson, who showed her a way of collecting twenty thousand dollars insurance so she could marry *him*."

"Mr. Mason, don't be silly! You were so nice, and now you're talking just like that district attorney."

"You don't know the half of it," Mason said. "Wait until you hear the way he's *going* to talk! You never have told me why you didn't take my advice and telephone the police when that body was discovered, and when that gun was still in your purse."

"Mr. Mason, I can't. I simply can't. I can't tell you that story. I can't tell anyone."

"All right," Mason said. "I can put on all sorts of a grandstand here, but you're going to be bound over for murder, and later on, unless you can tell some satisfactory story to a jury, you're going to be convicted of murder."

"Mr. Mason, can't *you* get me off?"

"Not unless I know what happened, and unless it's a good story."

"Other women shoot people and get off. Lawyers . . ."

"I know," Mason said, "but you're up against a different situation. Colson started masterminding this thing, and two men have been murdered. The revolver which killed one of them was in your possession both before and after the murders were committed. You're going to have one hell of a time explaining that it wasn't in your possession *while they were being committed.*"

"Mr. Mason, Arthur Colson wasn't the one who did what you call masterminding that."

"No?" Mason said skeptically. "He's never done anything, or said anything that convinced me of his sincerity."

She said impulsively, "He's simply trying to stand by me, Mr. Mason. You must believe that. You *must* understand that."

Mason merely smiled.

"The man who did what you call masterminding the thing," she said, "was someone whom you haven't even talked to."

"Who?"

"Willard Barton," she blurted, and then suddenly removed her gloved hand to press it against her lips. "There, I've said too much! He'd be furious if he knew that."

Mason watched her with coldly cynical eyes. "Was that an act?" he asked.

"What?"

"Letting that information slip out."

"No, I . . . I'm sorry I said it."

Mason said, "You're a damn smart little actress. I don't know what sort of trap you're setting for me now, but I'm not going to walk into it."

She said, "They can never *prove* that gun was in my possession if *you* keep quiet."

"What makes you think so?"

"Arthur Colson told me that."

Mason said angrily, "That dreamy-eyed goof!"

"He's smart, Mr. Mason. He's terribly clever."

"I daresay," Mason said sarcastically.

"And he says he won't ever let them trace that gun into my possession."

Mason said, "You were engaged to Hollister. He planned to leave on a business trip Monday night. You knew that and you spent that evening with Arthur Colson. I don't like that story, and the jury won't like it."

She said, "It's the truth. Arthur is just like a brother to me."

"Did Hollister know Arthur Colson?"

"No. They'd never met."

Mason said, "I don't like Arthur's presence in the case."

"You just wait," she flared. "He'll . . ."

Mason prompted as she paused, "He'll do what?"

"Nothing."

Mason studied her for a few seconds, then said, "That gun has my fingerprint on it. You're going to have to explain that eventually."

A cunning smile twitched the corners of her mouth. "Arthur Colson told me something about that. Don't worry, I'll explain it."

Chapter 27

As court reconvened, Hamilton Burger, still flushed and angry, but having regained some of his composure, said, "Call Willard Barton to the stand."

Lucille Barton, sitting at Mason's side, said under her breath in a whisper, "No, no. Don't let him do *that*."

Mason casually swung around in his chair. "Smile," he said.

There was panic in her eyes, her lips were trembling. "Smile," Mason ordered. "They're looking at you."

She twisted her lips in a quivering travesty of a smile.

Willard Barton, a well-groomed, chunky man with a profusion of dark, wavy hair which furnished a contrast with steel-gray eyes, settled himself in the witness chair in the manner of a substantial businessman who is more accustomed to giving orders than receiving them, and who is quite accustomed to being the center of attention.

In a firm, incisive tone he stated his name and address, gave his occuptation as that of an investor in potential oil-bearing properties, and then flashed Lucille the first quick glance he had given her since he had taken the stand. It was a glance of swift appraisal that held no emotion whatever. Then his eyes turned back to Hamilton Burger as he waited for the next question.

"You have the same name as the defendant in this case?"

"She has *my* name, yes, sir."

"You were married to her at one time?"

"Yes, sir."

"And divorced?"

"Yes."

"When were you divorced?"

"About eighteen months ago."

"The decree has become final?"

"It has."

"You are paying her alimony?"

"Yes, sir."

"Did you see her on the evening of the fifth of this month?"

"I did, yes, sir."

"What time?"

"About half-past six, perhaps a little later."

"Where?"

"I was at the Broadway Athletic Club. She telephoned me and asked if she could see me. I told her I'd see her for a moment in the lobby, but I warned her that if she tried to make any scene . . ."

"Objected to," Mason said. "Not responsive to the question which has already been asked and answered."

"Very well," Burger said irritably. "You saw her there in the lobby of the club?"

"I did, yes, sir."

"Who was present?"

"Just Lucille and I."

"What did she say?"

"She told me that something terrible had happened. That she was going to have to get out of the country. She wanted to know if I would give her fifteen thousand dollars in cash as a complete settlement if she'd waive any claims to future alimony payments and give me a complete release."

"You were paying her alimony?"

"Yes, sir."

"How much?"

"Two hundred dollars a week."

"Did she tell you why she wanted to leave the country?"

"Yes, sir."

"Why?"

"She said a man had been found dead in her garage. She finally admitted to me the body was that of her first husband, and said the exposure of that fact would ruin her."

"What did you tell her?"

"Well, naturally, I was trying to get out of paying any more than I had to. I told her I couldn't raise fifteen thousand dollars in cash. I told her I'd have to put her proposition up to my attorneys to see whether or not she could make a valid agreement under the circumstances. I told her I didn't think too much of the idea, and I thought the amount was too high."

"And did she accept that answer as final?"

"No, sir. She told me I'd have to do something fast. She said the offer wouldn't be open later than midnight. She said she would call me at a little before midnight. That she wanted to take a plane that night. Then, finally, she lowered her figure to ten thousand spot cash."

"Did she call you again?"

"No, sir. I had seen my attorneys and had made arrangements to accept her proposition, and I had the ten thousand dollars in cash, together with a proper release ready for her to sign. She didn't get in touch with me."

"And no one was with her when you saw her?"

"No, sir."

"Do you know a woman named Anita Jordon?"

"I have met her."

"Was she with the defendant when this conversation took place?"

"No, sir. The defendant was alone."

"Cross-examine," Burger said, hurling the words at Perry Mason as though they were a challenge.

"You were paying her two hundred dollars a week alimony?" Mason asked.

"Yes, sir."

"And you want the Court to believe that you hesitated

about the advisability of settling such weekly payments for fifteen thousand dollars?"

"Well, no, sir, I let *her* think I was hesitating."

"In other words, you told her you were hesitating, is that it?"

"I wanted to convey that impression, yes."

"But you actually were eager to make the settlement?"

"Naturally."

"But as a good business trader you tried to keep her from seeing that was your attitude."

"Yes, sir."

"So you told her that you didn't know whether you wanted to do it or not?"

"That's right."

"In other words, you lied to her."

Burton flushed.

Burger, on his feet, said, "Your Honor, I object to that. That's an insulting statement to the witness."

"Oh, I'll put it this way," Mason said, "if you'd like a softer term for the same thing. In other words, Mr. Barton, you told your wife a falsehood. Is that correct?"

Barton's eyes glinted angrily.

"Same objection," Burger said.

"It can be answered yes or no," Mason said.

Barton glared angrily at him.

"The question," Mason said, "is whether you told your wife a falsehood. It can be answered yes or no."

"About what?"

"About your willingness to make a settlement."

"I don't think that's material."

"I do," Mason said.

"Well, I don't," Hamilton Burger said. "I want to interpose an objection on that ground. It's not proper cross-examination."

"Overruled," Judge Osborne said.

"You told her a falsehood?" Mason asked.

"Yes," Barton shouted angrily.

"How long have *you* known Pitkin?"

"Well, I'd seen him but I didn't know who he was. That is, I had no idea he had ever been married to Lucille. It came as a shock to me when I realized that."

"But you had seen Pitkin?"

"I had known him as Mr. Argyle's chauffeur. Mr. Argyle is a member of the club to which I belong. Many oil men join it."

"And because you were interested in oil speculations, and Mr. Argyle, Mr. Ross P. Hollister, and Mr. Dudley Gates were all interested in similar transactions, and all members of the same club, you saw quite a bit of each other?"

"No, sir. Argyle, Hollister, and Gates had some sort of a partnership arrangement. They had pooled their interests in certain leases. While I was in the same general line of business, my own interests were adverse. I didn't want them to find out what I was doing. They didn't want me to find out what they were doing. We spoke when we met and occasionally would discuss general conditions, but we had very little in common."

"Had you ever spoken to Pitkin?"

"I had, but it was purely a personal matter."

"Trying to get Pitkin to tell you something about the business activities of the other three men?"

Burger shouted angrily, "Your Honor, that's another insulting question. It's utterly uncalled for."

"Do you have any evidence indicating such is the case, Mr. Mason?" Judge Osborne asked.

"No, Your Honor," Mason said, smoothly, "that question is merely part of a fishing expedition."

"The objection is sustained," Judge Osborne said. "You can, however, ask him what he discussed with Pitkin."

"What did you discuss with Pitkin? What was your reason for talking to him?"

Barton, thoroughly angry, said, "I wanted to hire a chauffeur by the day. I understood there was an association, sort of an employment agency, which specialized in that sort of stuff. I asked Pitkin about it because I knew he was Argyle's chauffeur. I happened to see him waiting out in front of the building. I asked him if he knew of such an association."

"Did he?"

"He did. He told me where it was. It was the Chauffeurs' Exchange. I believe it's listed in the telephone book. It's composed of chauffeurs who are willing to work on their days off. It's some sort of a mutual cooperative affair. They rotate jobs, and a person can nearly always get a chauffeur by the hour, or by the day, by calling up."

"Did Mr. Pitkin belong to that association?"

"He said he did. I don't know. He told me Thursday was his regular day off, that he was off duty at six o'clock Wednesday evening, and didn't have to come back until Friday morning. He said he'd be glad to take care of my needs himself on his days off, or I could get a chauffeur through the association on other days."

Mason said, "You have no affection left for your ex-wife, the defendant in this case?"

"I am very fond of Lucille in a way."

"And, trying to be clever, you advised her to plant a gun by the body of this man so it would look like suicide and say nothing to anyone, didn't you?"

"I did not. You have no proof of that. The defendant might make such a claim, but it's preposterous. Your accusation, sir, is entirely false, and is resented as such."

"Didn't you offer her *any* suggestion by which she might get out of the scrape in which she found herself?"

"Certainly not."

"Yet you say you are fond of her?"

"Yes."

"But you regarded that alimony settlement as a purely cold-blooded business transaction?"

"No, sir. I take an interest in Lucille. I wanted to be certain that she wasn't trying to raise money just to throw it away."

Mason said suavely, "Yet the affection which you bore for your ex-wife, the friendship, the regard, and the desire to see that she wasn't fleeced by some designing person, didn't prevent you from attempting to fleece her by deceiving her so that you could get a five thousand dollar advantage?"

"I don't think I had any idea of deceiving her."

"Then why did you try to conceal your eagerness to make a cash settlement such as she proposed?"

Barton thought that over, then said, "Well, just as a matter of habit I guess. Just as a matter of business policy."

"Come, come," Mason said. "You knew what you were doing. You deliberately concealed your eagerness to make the settlement."

"That's been gone over a dozen different times," Hamilton Burger said.

Judge Osborne said, "Well, I think counsel is entitled to make his point. It indicates the motivation of the witness and enables the Court to make an appraisal of the witness's character."

"All right," Barton suddenly shouted, "I lied to her! I saw a chance to make a good business deal. I tried to put it across. Now what's wrong with that?"

"Not a thing," Mason said, "and thank you very much for your commendable frankness, Mr. Barton. Now there's one other matter. As I understand your testimony, you say the defendant finally admitted the body was that of her first husband?"

"I don't think I said that."

Mason said, "I'll ask the court reporter to consult his notes and see what was said."

There followed a period of restless silence while the court reporter thumbed through the pages of his notes. Willard Barton changed his position on the witness stand.

"Here it is," the court reporter said. " '*Question:* Did she tell you why she wanted to leave the country? *Answer:* Yes, sir. *Question:* Why? *Answer:* She said a man had been found dead in her garage. She finally admitted to me the body was that of her first husband and said the exposure of that fact would ruin her.' "

Mason said, "Thank you, Mr. Court Reporter. I'll now ask you, Mr. Barton, what you meant when you said she '*finally admitted*' the body was that of her first husband?"

"Well, she finally admitted it, that's all."

"Not at first?"

"No."

"After searching questions on your part?"

"Yes, I guess so."

"So you discussed the matter and you felt she was trying to hold something back and kept questioning her?"

"I presume so."

"And in order to get her to '*finally admit*' what she did, you had to use some pressure?"

"Well, in a way."

"And you told her you couldn't help her unless she told you the truth, or words to that effect?"

"Yes, I guess so."

"So she told you the truth—finally?"

"Yes."

"So then you set about helping her?"

"I did not!"

"But you've already said you told her you couldn't help her unless she told the truth, and that because of your promise she '*finally admitted*' the truth. Now am I to understand *you* then failed to fulfill *your* part of the bargain?"

Barton hesitated, crossed his legs, glanced pleadingly at Burger.

"Well?" Mason demanded.

"I didn't *help* her," Barton blurted.

"That's what I thought," Mason said scornfully. "That's all, Mr. Barton."

Barton came down off the witness stand, swung over toward Mason's table, caught the cold, stony glint of the lawyer's eyes, thought better of what he had in mind, and veered away.

"Call Arthur Colson," Burger said, ignoring Barton.

Arthur Colson marched to the witness stand. His eyes moved restlessly around, appraising the courtroom, carefully avoiding, however, the eyes of the district attorney and the table behind which Mason and Lucille Barton sat.

He gave his name, age, occupation, and residence.

Hamilton Burger produced the gun. "I show you a .38 caliber Smith and Wesson revolver number S65088 and ask you if you ever saw that gun before?"

Colson took a sheet of paper from his pocket and reading from it, said, "I refuse to answer that question upon the ground that the answer might tend to incriminate me."

"Did you buy that gun from the Rushing Creek Mercantile Company?"

"I refuse to answer on the ground that the answer might tend to incriminate me."

"Did you sign the name Ross P. Hollister on the register?"

"I refuse to answer, same ground."

"Did you kill Hartwell L. Pitkin?"

"No."

"Did you know him?"

"No, sir. I didn't know him."

"Did you place this gun by the body of Hartwell L. Pitkin in the garage at number 719 South Gondola on the fifth of this month?"

"No, sir."

"Or at any other time?"

"No, sir."

"That's all," Hamilton Burger said.

"Just a minute," Mason said. "One more question on cross-examination. Did you ever have this gun in your possession?"

"I refuse to answer on the ground that the answer might incriminate me."

"Did you ever take it when Lucille Barton didn't know you had taken it?"

"I refuse to answer on the ground that the answer might incriminate me."

"Did you ever have a key to Lucille Barton's apartment?"

"No, sir."

Mason said, "I show you two letters, both typewritten, one of them addressed to the Drake Detective Agency, the other addressed to me. The first letter refers to a key to the apartment of Lucille Barton. The second letter refers to a key to the desk in that apartment. I ask you if you wrote either of those letters."

"No, sir. I did not."

"That's all," Mason said.

"That's all," Burger announced.

Judge Osborn said, "In view of the very unsatisfactory answers given upon such a vital point by the witness, the Court feels that the district attorney's office should take steps to clarify the situation."

"Yes, Your Honor," Burger said, wearily. "We are fully aware of the possibilities."

"And the implications," Judge Osborn said.

"And the implications," Burger repeated.

"Very well," Judge Osborn said. "Do you have one more witness you wish to put on before the hour of adjournment?"

"If the Court please, Your Honor, I'd like to wait until. . ."

"Very well. Court will now take a recess until two o'clock this afternoon. The defendant is remanded to the custody of the sheriff. Witnesses under subpoena are instructed to return here at two o'clock this afternoon."

As the spectators arose to leave the courtroom, Mason beckoned Paul Drake over to him. "Afraid I can't join you for lunch, Paul."

"Why, Perry?"

"I'm going to have to spend a couple of hours on the telephone. You take Della to lunch and get her a nice steak."

"Have a heart," Drake protested, grinning.

"I have," Mason told him, "and it's been in my mouth so long that I won't feel right when it drops back to where it belongs."

Chapter 28

At two o'clock when court reconvened, Hamilton Burger, apparently worried, said, "Your Honor, a peculiar situation has developed in this case. I had every reason to believe that it would be possible to connect this murder weapon with Mr. Perry Mason by reason of his fingerprint, and with the defendant by reason of the fact that I expected to be able to show Mr. Mason was with her at the garage at about the hour the man must have been murdered. That identification evidence has been made a football because of certain ingenious legal trickery, but I want to call to the Court's attention that it is merely an ingenious legal trickery. The witness ordinarily would have made an absolute identification."

"Well, of course," Judge Osborn said, "that's the vice of identification evidence. The witness saw a tall man wearing a light tan topcoat and a gray hat. He didn't see the man's face except vaguely and at a distance. A great number of men would answer that description. The description of the woman, because of the identification of her wearing apparel, which is more unusual, is, of course, much more persuasive; but there were probably thousands of tall men wearing light topcoats in the city at the hour the witness, Goshen, saw the couple at the garage."

"But there's only one Perry Mason who could have left a fingerprint on the inside of that gun belonging to his client," Burger said.

"You haven't proved the weapon belonged to his client yet," Judge Osborn said.

Hamilton Burger said, "I admit, Your Honor, the case has become somewhat complicated, but if the Court will bear with me I think the Court should appreciate the trickery by which the identification witness was confused."

Judge Osborn smiled. "The Court will bear with you as long as you're putting on proof, Mr. Burger."

"Very well. Call Sadie Milford."

Sadie Milford, a well-upholstered woman in the early forties, proved to be the manager of the apartment house where Lucille Barton had her apartment. She testified that the garages went with the apartments. That they were kept locked. That the apartment at 208 was entitled to a garage. That duplicate keys to the apartment and to the garage had been given Lucille Barton when she moved in.

"Who had these keys?"

"Lucille Barton."

"Do you have any receipt showing that to be the case?"

"Yes, sir."

"Was that signed by Lucille Barton?"

"Yes, sir."

"In your presence?"

"Yes, sir."

"I want it introduced in evidence," Hamilton Burger said.

"No objection," Mason said.

"Do you care to cross-examine?"

"Yes."

Mason took the receipt, said, "And you did deliver Lucille Barton these four keys, two to the apartment, and two to the garage?"

"Yes."

Burger's next witness was a service-station operator who testified that at a little after six o'clock on the evening of the fifth Lucille Barton had driven her automobile into the service station. It was a Chevrolet sedan with a light brown body. He had found the timing so out of adjustment that the car constantly skipped and backfired. He had changed the adjustment of the timing device, and while with the time and the tools available he hadn't been able to make a thoroughly workmanlike job of it, he had smoothed the car out so that it ran without backfiring.

"What time did she drive the car in there?" Hamilton Burger asked.

"About six-fifteen, or six-twenty."

"Who was driving it?"

"Miss Barton."

"Had you seen her before?"

"Yes, she buys gasoline from me regularly."

"And by Miss Barton you mean the defendant sitting there at the counsel table with Mr. Mason?"

"Yes, sir."

"That's all," Burger said.

"That's all," Mason announced, smiling. "No questions."

"Call Stephen Argyle," Burger said.

Argyle took the stand, gave his residence as 938 West Casino Boulevard, his age as fifty-five, stated that he had employed Hartwell L. Pitkin during his lifetime as chauffeur, and that Pitkin had been in his employ on the day of his death.

"When was the last time you saw Mr. Pitkin?" Burger asked.

"Shortly after five o'clock."

"Where was he at that time?"

"In front of the office of Mr. Perry Mason. That is, in front of the building where Mr. Mason has his office. I was waiting to see Perry Mason. I suddenly remembered that it was Hartwell's night off. Despite the fact that I was thoroughly annoyed with him, I went down and told him he could take the car and go home."

"And do you know what happened after that?"

"I only know that I found the car at my residence when I returned there."

"What time?"

"Sometime . . . oh, it was after I got back from calling on a patient in the hospital where I made an adjustment and . . ."

"Never mind anything about *that* case," Hamilton Burger said.

"Well, I was defrauded by Mr. Perry Mason into making settlement that cost me several thousand dollars," Argyle snapped.

"That's neither here nor there," Burger said, soothingly. "Just try to control yourself and tell us what happened."

"Well, it must have been around nine-thirty or ten o'clock when I returned home. The car was there."

"You may cross-examine," Burger said.

"How do you know it was there?" Mason asked.

"Why it . . . it had to be there. The garage door was closed . . ."

"But you didn't *look* for the car as soon as you returned home."

"No."

"How did you get home, by the way?"

"My companion drove me home, an adjuster for the insurance company which carries my insurance."

"You arrived home when?"

"Somewhere around nine-thirty or ten o'clock."

"And went to bed at what time?"

"Oh, I would say around eleven."

"And when did you have occasion to look in the garage for the car?"

"About two o'clock the next morning. I received a call on the telephone and the police told me about what had happened to my chauffeur. They asked me questions and said they were coming out. I got up and dressed, and was headed for the garage about the time the police arrived."

"Your car was in the garage?"

"That's right."

Mason said, "You evidenced some animosity toward me, Mr. Argyle."

"Personally," Argyle said, "I think you're beneath contempt."

"Why?"

"You knew that I had reason to believe my chauffeur had been in an automobile accident. You talked me into making a settlement of a claim which was entirely spurious. I warn you, Mr. Mason, I am going to sue you for fraud and . . ."

"Oh, it was your chauffeur whom you thought was driving the car?"

"Naturally. I knew I wasn't driving it. However, I was legally liable for the acts of my employee."

"Is this all material?" Judge Osborn asked.

"I think it shows motivation and bias on the part of the witness," Mason said.

"Let's go into it by all means," Burger announced, rubbing his hands. "I'd like now to show the entire facts."

Mason said, "You shall have the entire facts, Mr. Burger. Suppose you tell your side of the story, Mr. Argyle."

Argyle said, "Around three o'clock on the afteroon of the fifth, Mr. Mason came to my house. Mr. Pitkin was present at the interview. Mr. Mason stated that he had indisputable evidence that my car had been engaged in a hit-and-run accident in which a client of his had been seriously injured. He pointed out that there were bumps on the fenders of my car and . . . well, I thought he was right."

"Why did you think I was right?" Mason asked.

"Because my chauffeur had been in trouble with the car on that date. He'd tried to get rid of it and had reported it as being stolen. He had advised me the car had been stolen and insisted I join him so he could explain the circumstances to the police. I went with him to the place where he said he had left the car. The man had been drinking and seemed terribly nervous about something. I was skeptical but badly worried myself, fearing my man might have been in some scrape which would involve me. I returned to my club and telephoned the police that my car had been stolen. Actually I don't think the car was ever stolen at all. It was recovered by the police in the downtown business district where it had been parked in front of a fireplug."

Mason said, "And on the strength of what I had told you, you decided that it would be cheaper for you to hunt up Finchley and make a settlement behind his attorney's back, didn't you?"

"I didn't think any such thing."

"But that's exactly what you *did*, isn't it?"

"As soon as I realized a man had been seriously hurt I naturally wanted to do something about it. I felt very much concerned about the whole thing. I went to your office. I kept trying to see you. You were out—apparently calling on your client, Lucille Barton."

"Do you know that?" Mason asked.

"No, I don't know it."

"Have you any reason to think that's where I was?"

"Well, I understood from the police . . . I'll withdraw that. The answer is no, I don't *know.*"

"All right," Mason said. "You were at my office and were told I was out."

"Yes."

"And where was your chauffeur then?"

"Sitting in my Buick automobile in front of your office building, waiting."

"You had found a parking place there?"

"My chauffeur had. He had let me out at the entrance to the building. There were no parking places available near the building. I told him to keep driving around the block until he found a parking place right near the entrance of the building. He located one almost immediately."

"So you were waiting for me?"

"Yes, sir, until I telephoned my insurance carrier about six o'clock and told him I was trying to make a settlement with you on a claim for damages. I had suddenly wakened to a realization that I might be negligent in not reporting to my insurance company."

"And the insurance carrier suggested to you that you could make a lot cheaper settlement by going out and making a settlement behind my back."

"My insurance carrier told me to wait there in the lobby and not to talk to you under any circumstances, until I had seen him. After he arrived, I placed the matter in his hands."

"But you *did* go to the hospital and try to make a settlement with my client behind my back, didn't you?"

"I don't know what you mean by behind your back. You weren't in your office. I certainly tried to communicate with you. I'm not going to wait all day for a lawyer, who's out gallivanting around with a divorcée, to get back to his office. *My* time's valuable!"

"Now, when you made that settlement," Mason said, "You paid out some money of your own in addition to the settlement made by the insurance company, didn't you?"

"Yes, I did."

"Why did you do that?"

"Because I thought the young man was entitled to more money than the insurance company was giving him. I'm not exactly a philanthropist, but on the other hand, I don't have to make my money by capitalizing on the suffering of a young boy."

"Very noble sentiments," Mason said, "but do you want this Court to understand that you not only told your insurance carrier you were liable, but paid out this money of yours purely on the strength of my statement to you that your car had been involved in an accident?"

"Well, I thought you were a reputable attorney. I know

different now. At the time, when you said you had proof—well, I thought you had it."

Mason grinned. "Very, very noble and self-righteous, Mr. Argyle. But despite the fact you now consider me beneath contempt, you did go to the doorman of your club and bribe him to swear you hadn't left the club that afternoon so *you* wouldn't be mixed up in anything your chauffeur might have done."

"That's not so!"

"You did give the doorman some money?"

"A tip is all."

"How much?"

"That's neither here nor there."

"How much?"

"Objected to, Your Honor," Burger said, jumping up. "this man was deliberately victimized by . . ."

"Overruled," Judge Osborn snapped.

"How much?" Mason asked.

"Well, I *thought* I was giving him five dollars, but I had had a couple of drinks and it was dark. And later on I was short in my cash, so I may have made a mistake and given him more."

"A hundred dollars?"

"I am afraid so."

"By mistake?"

"By mistake."

"You knew *you* hadn't been driving the car on the afternoon of the third."

"Yes, sir."

"Then you knew then that the only other person who could have done so was your chauffeur."

"Well, the car *could* have been stolen."

"In which event you wouldn't have been liable for an accident," Mason said. "Come, Mr. Argyle, you're a businessman."

"Well," Argyle said, "I see what you're getting at. As a

matter of fact, after you left, I put the thing up to my chauffeur and he broke down and virtually admitted that he had been driving the car and had been involved in that hit-and-run case. Then he admitted he had tried to avoid liability by telling me the car had been stolen."

"Exactly," Mason said. "Now you have come to the conclusion that statement was false?"

"You mean your statement to me that my car was involved in the hit-and-run accident?"

"Put it that way if you want to."

"That statement was absolutely and utterly false. A man by the name of Caffee was driving the car that hit that young boy."

Mason said, "By the way, you and the representative of the insurance company went to Mr. Finchley and threatened to prosecute him for obtaining money under false pretenses unless he returned the money you'd paid him, didn't you?"

"Well, we explained to him that he certainly wasn't entitled to the money either by law or equity."

"What did he say?"

"He said that you'd advised him to keep the money. That it was a voluntary payment and that we couldn't get it back. That you were going to teach these insurance adjusters not to suck eggs."

Judge Osborn smiled broadly.

"Exactly," Mason said. "Now why do you suppose Mr. Pitkin admitted to you he had been engaged in this hit-and-run accident if he actually hadn't?"

"I don't know," Argyle said, "and I wish I did. I've been thinking it over, trying to find the answer to it, and I simply can't figure it out. It now would seem the man was a blackmailer. He doubtless had some reason in that warped mind of his."

Mason said, "You were anxious to see that your chauffeur had his night off, despite the fact that he had just confessed to you he had been engaged in a hit-and-run driving accident?"

"I can explain that."

"Go ahead and do so."

"I knew my chauffeur made money on his days and nights off. He had explained to me that he was a member of this chauffeurs' association and that they worked on their days off, and I knew that it was important that he get up to that association because they make definite bookings. I'm a businessman myself. I knew how I'd feel if I should be waiting for a chauffeur who didn't show up on time. Letting Pitkin go wasn't out of consideration for him, but to his associates in the chauffeurs' association."

"Now then," Mason said, "has it ever occurred to you that that's exactly what did happen, Mr. Argyle?"

"What do you mean?"

"That Pitkin had some definite obligation. Someone for whom he was to work on the evening of the fifth. That in place of taking your car home himself, he made arrangements with some other individual to take it home, and that *he* went out at once to work on this assignment to which he had obligated himself."

Argyle paused to think that over, then said, "It could be that such is the case."

Mason said, "Did *you* ever have occasion to hire any of these chauffeurs on Pitkin's day off?"

"Certainly not. If I had wanted to do that, I'd have simply made arrangements with Pitkin to have charged me the regular rate for working overtime, and kept him."

Mason said, "I'm going to hand you a list of fifteen names and ask you if you know any one of those people, Mr. Argyle."

"Oh, what's the use of this?" Hamilton Burger expostulated.

Mason said, "It may explain the reason the chauffeur,

Pitkin, confessed he had been in a hit-and-run accident when he actually hadn't."

"Oh, very well," Burger said. "I don't see the point. It seems to me, Your Honor, we're not only not getting anywhere with this cross-examination, but that it's just a general fishing expedition."

"Fishing in promising waters, however," the Court said, smiling. "I think perhaps Mr. Mason is even getting an occasional nibble."

Argyle adjusted his glasses, looked at the typewritten list, scratched his head, said, "It's going to take me a few minutes to check this list over, Mr. Mason."

"Very well," Judge Osborn said. "The Court will take a fifteen-minute recess. You can look at the list during that time, Mr. Burger, and discuss it with the witness. Court will recess for fifteen minutes."

Judge Osborn returned to chambers.

Mason got up, stretched, yawned with elaborate carelessness, walked over to where Lieutenant Tragg was sitting, and said, "How about stepping over here in the corner for a few minutes, Lieutenant?"

Tragg nodded, and the two men moved over to a corner of the courtroom.

Tragg grinned surreptitiously, and said, "Thanks for your cross-examination of Holcomb. He's been boasting all over about how he trailed you to a place where Goshen could identify you after I'd fallen down on the job. I guess this will cause him to change his tune a little. Not that I am talking to you officially, you understand, Mason, this is just personal."

"Sure," Mason said. "And still talking personally, how'd you like to take a ride, Tragg?"

"Where?"

"Out to the residential district."

"Do you think we have time?"

"I think we have lots of time," Mason said.

"We can't get out there and back inside of fifteen minutes, can we?"

"I think," Mason said, "that when Argyle sees that list he's going to want a little more time. He . . . here comes Burger now."

Hamilton Burger, moving with the ponderous dignity of a man who is forced by business exigencies to consult with someone for whom he has a contemptuous hatred, said, "How important is that list of witnesses, Mason?"

"Quite important."

"Argyle can't possibly check them until he checks a list of some of his stockholders. He says he has a poor memory for names, but he thinks nearly all these men are stockholders in one of his companies. If you want an answer to that question, the case will have to go over until tomorrow morning."

"Suits me," Mason said.

"Well, it doesn't suit me," Burger said.

"I want an answer to the question," Mason insisted.

"Well," Burger announced after some hesitancy, "very well. On your stipulation, we'll let it go over until tomorrow morning."

"Will you explain to the judge?" Mason asked.

"Very well," Burger said, and swung around on his heel.

"Now," Mason said to Tragg, "if you are ready to go, Lieutenant—and I think we'd better take your car."

"Say, do you know what you're doing?" Tragg asked.

"I hope so," Mason told him.

Chapter 29

Tragg backed his car into the mouth of the alley Mason indicated.

"We can see the house from here," Mason said.

"Just what are you getting at?" Tragg asked.

Mason said, "Hollister started out on a business trip, didn't he?"

"That's right."

"And intended to be gone for several days?"

"Yes."

"When you found the car and the body," Mason said, "there were certain significant things you didn't find."

"What do you mean?"

"Baggage. When a man intends to go on a trip he takes baggage with him."

"That's right," Tragg said.

"Now, the body was in a peculiar position," Mason pointed out. "What does that position indicate to you, Lieutenant?"

"Only one thing," Tragg said. "The body must have been jammed into the trunk of an automobile."

"That's right. Now was that the trunk of Hollister's automobile?"

"It could have been."

"Here comes Argyle. Driving pretty fast, isn't he, Lieutenant?"

Tragg said, "He probably has a lot of things on his mind. I imagine this trial has disrupted his program."

Mason stretched, yawned, said, "I suppose so."

"What do we do now?" Tragg asked.

"Just wait," Mason said. "You have your radio on here?"

"Yes."

Mason said, "Better make sure it's in working order. Check in to Headquarters and get the time."

Tragg said, "What the devil are you getting at, Mason? What's the idea?"

Mason said, "It suddenly occurred to me I'd taken you away rather unceremoniously. Burger may be trying to get in touch with you. I suppose the blowup of that identification business . . ."

Tragg grinned, and said, "Boy, that *was* pretty! I don't mind telling you, Mason, I wanted to jump up and cheer— personally, you understand, not officially."

Tragg tuned in his radio, checked with police headquarters, settled back and lit a cigar. "Mason, what the devil are we waiting for? If you want to see Argyle why not go over and see him?"

"Oh, let's let him get his records together if that's what he wants. He . . . here he comes now."

Argyle came out of the front door almost on the run, carrying a handbag in one hand, a suitcase in the other. He slammed them in the car and started the motor.

"Now," Mason said, "if you'll start closing in on him, Lieutenant, and use your siren, I think we may get some action."

"Use the siren!" Tragg exclaimed. "What's *he* done?"

"Follow him and you'll see what he's *going* to do," Mason said. "He'll at least give you a chance to catch him for speeding."

"Damn it," Tragg, "I'm not a traffic cop. I . . ."

"Do you want this deal or don't you?" Mason asked.

Tragg looked at him sharply, said, "Okay, I do."

"Better get going then."

Tragg started the motor, eased the police car into gear, slid in the clutch, and started after Argyle's car.

After a moment he poured more throttle into the big police car, said, "That guy certainly is going!"

"What's the limit along here?" Mason asked.

"Thirty-five miles," Tragg said. "He's hitting better than fifty. He shouldn't do that."

"Try giving him the siren," Mason said.

Tragg said, "Well, we'll get alongside of him and . . . ."

"Give him the siren," Mason said impatiently, and threw in the switch which started the siren wailing.

Tragg hurriedly kicked the switch out, said, "Damn it, don't do that. I . . ."

Argyle looked back, a startled apprehensive glance, saw the police car coming behind him, and suddenly floorboarded the throttle, sending his car into speed.

"What do you make of that?" Lieutenant Tragg said. "Why, the damn fool, he's . . . hell, Mason, he's trying to get away!"

"Of course he's trying to get away," Mason said. "What are *you* going to do about it?"

"I'll show you," Tragg said grimly. He threw the siren on.

Argyle screamed into a sudden turn to the left, almost upsetting as he skidded around the corner.

"Hold everything," Tragg said, grimly. "You're going to travel."

He slammed the car into second gear, poured the thottle to it and sent the car around the corner in a screaming skid, then snapped it back into high.

"Learned that in the old bootlegging days," he said.

"He's going to try another turn," Mason said.

"We'll cure him of that," Tragg said. "A good cop can take the turns a lot faster than . . . hold your hat, Mason, here we go again."

Tragg sent the car into another screaming turn, which left black tire marks all over the highway.

"I guess he'll try the straightaway now," Mason said. "Better get your gun handy, Tragg. He may want to shoot it out."

"What the hell's he running away from?" Tragg asked.

"The murder of Hartwell L. Pitkin, and the murder of Ross P. Hollister," Mason told him, lighting a cigarette. "How about . . ."

Tragg threw a switch in the radio, said, "Calling Headquarters. Lieutenant Tragg, car number forty-two. I'm chasing a murder suspect in a black Buick sedan, number 9Y6370 north of Hickman Avenue, between Eighty-ninth and Ninetieth Street. Send any available squad cars to help. I have my siren going."

Tragg eased his gun around in his holster. "You got a gun, Mason?"

"I'm a law-abiding citizen," Mason told him.

"You're deputized," Tragg said tersely. "There's a gun in the glove compartment. Get it. Do you really have the dope on this guy?"

"Of course I have the dope on him," Mason said. "Otherwise we wouldn't be wasting time but I couldn't prove it until he started running. I had to get him stampeded so he'd give himself away."

"He's sure doing it now," Tragg said, gripping the wheel. "We're hitting eighty miles an hour "

"He's going to get away on the straightaway," Mason said.

"My siren is really clearing the way for him," Tragg said, "but if I shut it off, we'll hit somebody and we'll all be killed."

Mason said, "Just keep your siren going, Lieutenant. We can get him sooner or later and this flight is the last nail in his coffin. He . . . *look out!*"

A car shot out of an intersecting street, heard the scream

of the siren, saw Argyle's car and Tragg's car rushing along the highway, and tried to swing back to the curb.

Argyle swerved to avoid a collision. His car went into a skid, started rocking dangerously, then suddenly spun completely around, went up on two wheels, shot across the road, over an embankment, and turned over.

Lieutenant Tragg slammed on his brakes.

Mason watched for a moment to see if Argyle emerged from the wreckage, then said, "I guess that does it, Lieutenant. I take it I'm no longer a deputy."

With that he opened the glove compartment and returned the revolver to its holster.

Chapter 30

Paul Drake, Della Street, and Perry Mason relaxed in Mason's private office. Della Street, perched on a corner of the desk, held one knee in her interlaced fingers. Mason was tilted back in his swivel chair and Drake was sprawled in his customary sideways position in the big clients' chair.

"You mean you knew who it was all along?" Drake asked.

"Of course not," Mason said, "but as soon as I knew that Argyle's car hadn't hit Finchley, I wondered why it was that Argyle would so willingly part with cold, hard cash to settle a claim for which he wasn't responsible. Then I began to wonder if he wasn't buying an alibi."

"Well, of course, it's plain enough now," Drake said, "but I'm darned if I see how you got it at the start."

Mason said, "Here's a pretty good reconstruction of what happened, Paul. Argyle, Hollister and Gates were associated in some oil deals. Hollister furnished most of the capital and took the largest share of the profits. Argyle and Gates started double-crossing Hollister. Hollister either caught them at it, or smelled a rat. He called a conference to take place at his home in Santa del Barra on Monday the third. Argyle and Gates very reluctantly drove up there."

"Did Pitkin drive them up?" Drake asked.

Mason grinned. "No, Pitkin was in San Francisco."

"I don't get it," Drake said.

"Gates and Argyle were in such a spot that they could have been sent to jail for embezzlement. Hollister finally had the goods on them. Gates knew it. Argyle only

222

suspected it. Gates had decided that if it came to a showdown, he'd shoot his way out, if he had half a chance.

"So he'd purchased a plane ticket to Honolulu in his name. Then he paid Pitkin to travel the first leg of the journey *under his name*.

"That gave Gates an alibi in case he had to use one. And he put a .45 automatic in his pocket so he'd be prepared.

"It was as bad as he thought. Hollister served his ultimatum, probably calling on the men to strip themselves of everything. It called for quick decision. Gates made it with his automatic.

"Argyle was almost crazy. Gates had had things all planned for what had to be done in case he killed Hollister. He whipped Argyle into line. They brought in waterproof canvas from the trunk of Gates' car, swiftly rolled the body into a bundle, carried it to the side door and slipped it into the trunk of Hollister's car.

"Then they drove both Argyle's car and Hollister's car up the canyon road. Gates outlined his alibi to Argyle, but Argyle realized he was left without an alibi. Gates told him to rush back to his club and report his car as having been stolen. That was to protect them in case anyone had seen them on the grade. They then smashed Hollister's wrist watch with the hands registering 5:55, and the car clock with the hands at 6:21. Then they parked Argyle's car, drove up to where they could turn Hollister's car around, rolled the body over the bank, shoved earth over it, then sent Hollister's car over a steep ledge and dashed back to Santa del Barra.

"Gates put his alibi into effect by using Hollister's name and calling for Gates at the San Francisco airport from Hollister's phone. Pitkin answered in the name of Gates. That clinched Gates' alibi.

"When Hollister was shot, the body fell on a thick, expensive but small Oriental rug. The two murderers had no time to clean the rug and replace it. So they removed the rug so the bloodstains wouldn't betray them when the house-keeper came to work the next morning. She knew Hollister was intending to take a business trip so she thought nothing of his absence, but she did wonder what had happened to the rug. The day previous, Hollister had mentioned something about giving a rug to Lucille for her apartment. The housekeeper wired Lucille, asking if Hollister had given her the Oriental rug. Lucille became angry, replied that she had the rug Hollister had intended she should have. The house-keeper didn't think much about it until after Hollister's body was found.

"Argyle rushed back here. Pitkin returned by plane. Gates flew to San Franciso, picked up the ticket Pitkin had left for him and went on to Honolulu. Pitkin was smart enough to know he hadn't been paid a large chunk of money to build an alibi for nothing. From that moment he decided to find out why and collect blackmail—and Argyle decided to kill Pitkin.

"Argyle went to his club, reported his car as having been stolen and tried to bribe an alibi. As soon as he calmed down he knew that was a poor way to do it.

"Then Argyle saw our ad in the *Blade* and conceived the idea of buying himself a real alibi by pretending he'd been the hit-and-run driver. He felt he could square that rap and make the insurance company stand most of the expense.

"In searching Hollister's body, Argyle had found keys to Lucille Barton's apartment and garage. He must have known Hollister was going to marry her and what the whole relationship was.

"When Argyle saw your ad in the *Blade* he realized that if he could pose as the driver of the hit-and-run car, he could pay off the claims, mostly with money furnished by the insurance company, and have a perfectly swell alibi. Obviously, if he had been at the intersection of Hickman Avenue and Vermesillo Drive at five P.M. on the evening of the third, he couldn't have been in Santa del Barra at the time the murder was committed. Remember that he *did* have a good alibi for the rest of the evening. He saw to that. Hollister's housekeeper had left at four-thirty on the afternoon of the third. Hollister was alive then and had told the housekeeper he was going to have a short conference and then leave on a business trip.

"Argyle went about killing Pitkin with calm deliberation and considerable shrewdness. He sent a letter to you, enclosing a key to Lucille's apartment. He felt certain that would send someone out to talk with him. He had a new right rear wheel put on his automobile, he dented the fender and had it covered with paint. Then he did the thing which was diabolically clever, the thing by which he intended to give himself an ironclad alibi for Pitkin's murder."

"What?" Drake asked. "If you ask me, he had an ironclad alibi. Hell, Perry, he was sitting in your office at the time the murder was committed."

Mason said, "He went to an employment agency sometime on the fifth, hired a chauffeur, and arranged to pick him up, to have him start work shortly before five o'clock in the afternoon. He explained that this chauffeur would have to go to Detroit by bus in order to pick up a new automobile and drive it down to Mexico to meet him. In that way, the chauffeur would never read any of the papers about Pitkin's death.

"Argyle was smart enough to know that if a man wearing a chauffeur's cap and an overcoat should be seen sitting in his car, witnesses would naturally assume that the chauffeur was Pitkin. At least people who didn't know Pitkin.

"From the attitude Pitkin had toward Argyle, I am assuming Pitkin may have been trying to blackmail Argyle even before Hollister's murder. At any rate, Pitkin had become suspicious of the alibi he'd been building for Gates and wondered if Argyle wasn't in on it too. Argyle evidently had been investigating Pitkin. He'd found out that Pitkin was Lucille's first husband, that she was planning to marry Hollister and that she was out of the apartment from two to five each afternoon. As soon as he got the keys to Lucille's apartment he started planning the murder of Pitkin. My ad in the paper gave him what he doubtless felt was the opportunity of a lifetime. He started prowling in Lucille's apartment and when he found there was a gun in the desk he had everything just the way he wanted it.

"He got Pitkin down to Lucille's garage. Now, the interesting thing is that Pitkin didn't know where Lucille lived. When they went to the garage at 719 South Gondola, it probably meant nothing in the world to Pitkin. He had seen Lucille, knew she was in the city somewhere, and was trying to find her, but he didn't know where she lived.

"On some pretext, Argyle got Pitkin to monkey around with the timing on Lucille's automobile—and it's just possible he knew that Arthur Colson had been rewiring the car. Remember he'd been collecting data on Pitkin, Hollister and Lucille for some time. It was a very sweet setup for Argyle. He waited until the car was sputtering and backfiring so that the noise of the revolver shot would simply sound like one more backfire and wouldn't have any significance whatever to any person who might be listening. He simply pulled the trigger, pocketed the gun, stepped into Lucille's car, drove it across the street, and parked it at the curb. He left the keys in the car, put a fresh shell in the gun, then went up to Lucille's apartment and put the gun back in the desk. After that he got in his own car, drove out to pick up his new chauffeur, and was waiting in front of my office by the time Della arrived. He was careful enough to let the man at the cigar stand see *a* chauffeur driving the car around, looking for a parking place and eventually finding one. He had luck in that Della Street also noticed the car and chauffeur.

"He waited around for me as long as he dared. Then he rang up the insurance adjuster, who promptly told him not to have anything to do with me.

"The insurance adjuster came out and picked up Argyle. Argyle told him a story which scared the insurance company to death, offered to stand some of the settlement himself, and they went out to see Bob Finchley."

"How did Argyle know you found the desk locked on that first visit to Lucille's apartment?"

"He must have been waiting where he could watch the apartment. He saw me go in. After I'd left and Lucille had gone out, he found the desk was locked. When I did nothing about hunting him up he knew I hadn't got the license number he'd planted into the notebook, so he sent me a key to the desk, special messenger.

"You see Lucille went out as soon as I'd left so Arthur Colson could tell her what to say. She thought I might be setting a trap for her.

"And when Argyle saw her go out, all dolled up like a million dollars, he felt certain she was goind to see Colson. Argyle had previously made himself a duplicate key to the desk just in case.

"He dashed off a letter and sent me the key.

"There was Argyle's plan and it was a peach. If it hadn't been for the fact that our ad in the paper actually struck pay dirt in having Carlotta Boone come in and put the finger on Caffee, we never would have suspected anything.

"Now, notice the most suspicious circumstance of all, when you come right down to it. When I talked with Argyle on the afternoon of the fifth, he let it appear that *he* had been driving the car. He showed all of the evidences of guilt, and the same was true of the time he went to see Finchley. But after he realized we had found the real hit-and-run driver he started blaming it all on his chauffeur.

"You see he realized what a precarious position he was in, so he extricated himself by reporting a purely fictitious conversation with Pitkin."

"But didn't that leave him wide open?" Drake asked.

"Sure, but there was nothing else he *could* do. Of course, once he realized Hollister's housekeeper thought the missing rug had been given Lucille, Argyle felt greatly relieved. If it hadn't been for a mere fluke, Hollister's car might not have been found for months. And if the car hadn't been found the body wouldn't have been found.

"But the breaks were against Argyle on Hollister's death just as they were all in his favor on Pitkin's death.

"You see, Lucille didn't want to call the police until she had made a settlement with Willard Barton. He pried the truth out of her and suggested she plant the gun so it would look like suicide. Arthur Colson very agreeably used a small wheel to grind the numbers off of the gun. When Lucille saw the body of her ex-husband in the garage, she must have had at least a suspicion someone had taken her gun to do the job. Perhaps she noticed the desk had been ransacked in her absence. I'd emptied shells from the gun. They reloaded it, fired one shell and planted the gun in the garage."

"They must have worked fast on the Hollister job," Drake said.

"Sure. Gates had planned every detail, in case he had to shoot his way out. They arrived at Hollister's house about twenty minutes to five. Hollister was blunt and angry, Gates cold-blooded and deadly. Hollister was killed and rolled in canvas within a few minutes. After that it wasn't too great a job to do the rest of it. Argyle was back here by seven o'clock, and took care to have an alibi for the rest of the evening."

"How did you make Argyle crack?" Drake asked. "That's something I don't get."

"It was when I handed him that list of names," Mason said. "It was a cinch. During the noon hour I rang up every employment agency in town and asked them the names of all persons who had been hired to act as chauffeurs on the fourth or fifth of the month. I had a list of fifteen names which included men who had been hired as butlers and general handymen. I presented that list to Argyle. He saw on there the name of the man whom he had employed and who was even then on a bus, riding to Detroit. That hit him hard. He knew then that I knew."

"How did you ever get that Detroit angle?" Drake asked.

"I didn't have it at the time," Mason said. "At that time it was only a theory. Tragg checked the list after Argyle was removed from the wreck, taken to the hospital, and made a deathbed confession. He found one man—Orville Nettleton—who had given up his room, telling his landlady he had a job for a man who was going to send him to Detroit to pick up a new car and then drive it to Mexico, where his employer would meet him later on. The man was tickled pink over his job and mentioned the name of his new employer, Argyle."

"Well," Della Street said, "it was a nice case, but I don't see any fee in it."

"I'm afraid you won't," Mason said, grinning. "A lawyer occasionally has a case thrust upon him, and this is one we're going to have to charge to profit and loss."

Drake said, "It *should* teach you not to leave your fingerprints on guns."

"And to keep out of girls' apartments," Della Street added.

"You'll notice," Mason told them, grinning, "that I promptly surrendered the key to the apartment to Lieutenant Tragg."

"Gosh, yes," Drake said. "I wonder what Tragg's done with that key."

"Well," Della Street said, "you had *some* compensation, chief. You had a nice tête-à-tête and a breakfast with the much-married Lucille."

"Much-married, but cautious," Mason observed.

Drake winked at Della Street. "I wonder if Mason was also cautious?"

"*I* wonder," Della Street said.

"Keep wondering, both of you," Mason told them, grinning, "and remember that while I missed a fee in a murder case, I certainly made a killing on Finchley's case."

"Darned if you didn't," Drake admitted admiringly. "I certainly had to laugh when I saw Judge Osborn's face when the real nature of that deal dawned on him. Particularly when Argyle quoted Finchley as saying you were going to teach certain insurance adjusters not to suck eggs."

Mason said, "By the way, Paul, I saw your secretary as I came down the corridor. She said if you were in here to let you know that the client in the Emery case was anxious for a report."

Drake came up out of the chair with a sudden bound. "My gosh," he said, "I'd forgotten about Emery! Well, be good."

Mason watched the door slowly close.

"You certainly built a fire under him," Della Street said.

Mason nodded. "I thought," he said, "we could arrange for a congratulatory dinner, in celebration of squeezing out of a trap through a darn narrow opening, Della."

She glanced at him demurely. "Then why get rid of Paul Drake?"

"Because I didn't think we needed a chaperon."

"Sounds interesting," Della Street said.